STARWRECKED!

"You are on the Class Four Quarantined Planet of Quebahr," announced the lifeboat computer. "As a Quarantined World, Quebahr is barred from any knowledge of the Federation or of life beyond its atmosphere—and the Quarantine is of greater importance than the lives of any castaways. Efforts will be made to rescue you, subject to the Quarantine. Please maintain your disguise programming, native culture training and language briefing while on planet. Proceed to and activate the rescue beacon at the prestated location. After supplies are unloaded, this craft will self-destruct."

"Wait!" Jim cried. "You can't! *What* beacon? *What* disguises? *What* natives? We're not Federation citizens—*we haven't been trained*!"

In mute reply a hatch opened, jettisoning boxes. With a small noise and a small puff of smoke, the lifeboat blew up.

Jim, Ellen and Curt stared at each other. They were stranded on an unknown world; their one link to the mysterious Federation—and to Earth—was gone. And their Alien guide was in a state of comatose shock.

GORDON R. DICKSON

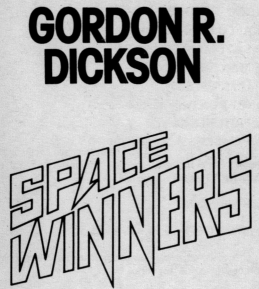

SPACE WINNERS

A TOM DOHERTY ASSOCIATES BOOK

SPACE WINNERS

Copyright © 1965 by Gordon R. Dickson

Reprinted by arrangement with Holt Rinehart and Winston

First TOR printing: January 1986

A TOR Book

Published by Tom Doherty Associates
49 West 24 Street
New York, N.Y. 10010

Cover art by Alan Gutierrez

ISBN: 0-812-53558-8
CAN. ED.: 0-812-53559-6

Printed in the United States of America

0 9 8 7 6 5 4 3 2 1

FOR
MY
MOTHER,
MAUDE L. DICKSON

SPACE WINNERS

1

It was a little, Jim Rawlins thought at last on Sunday night, like being the fastest gun west of Tombstone.

He had no liking for the reputation he had picked up, especially these last two years, for being stubborn. He tried to duck it. But somebody was always coming around to challenge him.

Sunday night, sitting out in the Rawlins carport, wrestling a rebuilt bearing into the gyrostabilizer of his motorbike, it had happened again. This time about odds. And with Ward Stuyler, who had been with him all through the last five years of junior and senior high school.

"You say it and then you take it back in the next breath!" Ward finally exploded. He was perched on a five-gallon oil can, watching Jim tap the bearing into place in the torn down gyro system.

"No, I don't," said Jim.

"But you admit nearly a million to one is long odds!" Ward yelled. "Then you turn around and say there'd be nothing impossible about being one of the three winners the Aliens'll pick from the continental U.S. testing area. *Three* out of nearly three million graduating high-school seniors!"

"I say it, because there wouldn't," said Jim, doggedly. "Practically impossible has to mean I can figure safely that for practical purposes something's not going to happen. But this *is* going to happen—for three people. For those three, like the seventeen other winners the Aliens are supposed to pick in the other testing areas around the world, it never was practically impossible."

"But—" Ward tried hard to break in, but Jim plowed ahead.

"—In fact," said Jim, "it was a cinch. Those three just happened to be the ones with the exact chance combination of talent and character that the Alien Federation's looking for. For the three we're talking about, then, it was certain from the start—they just didn't know it. And 'them' might include you, or me."

"There!" said Ward. "You said it yourself— *'Chance.'* Chance is luck, isn't it?"

"No," said Jim, scowling. "Anyway, not for me. It'd be bad luck."

"Sure, sure I know!" said Ward. "You've got your future all planned. So you wouldn't want to go."

"That's right," said Jim, stiffly.

"You must be the only one out of the entire three million who thinks that way; that's all I've got to say," said Ward. "Catch me turning it down if I was one of the ones picked! You know our area got its tests finished first—that means our three will probably be the first humans into interstellar space. Catch me turning down something like that! I'd come back to Earth full of Alien information no one else here on Earth knew, and be fixed for life. Anyway, you just admitted believing in luck."

"I didn't," Jim banged hard on the bearing ring, to seat it on the gyro shaft. "I don't believe in luck."

"Carry me home! I give up!" Ward tossed his arms wide and almost went over backward off the oil can. For a moment he teetered, then he got his feet back on the concrete beneath him. "What is it when you flip a coin and it can come up either heads or tails? Is that luck, or isn't it?"

"It isn't." Jim scowled again. "The side that's up when the coin lands depends on the lift and spin you gave it in flipping. If you could calculate those forces exactly, you could tell before it landed if it was going to be heads, or tails. Same way with lightning striking. If you could calculate all the factors, you could tell where it would hit. There's no such thing as luck, when you get right to it."

"What is there, then?" demanded Ward.

"The laws of cause and effect!" growled Jim. They ended up settling nothing.

"Oh, there you are," said Taub Widerman, as Jim came into Building B at Research Three the next morning and made his way through the maze of equipment and heavy power cables involved in Building B's part of the research. Weary-looking, probably from working to midnight the night before, Jim guessed, the young physicist ran a hand over his already balding forehead. "I was just going to start without you."

"The new bearing in my gyrostabilizer jammed on the way here," said Jim, apologetically.

His summer job at Research Three was taking care of the animals and fish used by Taub as experimental subjects. He had stopped on arriving at Building B only long enough to put on the swimming trunks that were his ordinary working uniform, but he saw now that Taub had been held up without him.

It was next to impossible for the physicist to direct the time-gap transmitter—his working tool—upon the experimental subjects, while at the same time handling the subjects themselves. But Taub, Jim saw, had been warming up the transmitter when Jim appeared. So it was high time Jim was here. Handling the subjects was Jim's job—one he hoped to keep on a part-time basis after he started at the university this coming fall.

"Something special, Taub?" he asked now. "You don't usually need me until I've finished cleaning the tanks and cages."

"Visitors today," replied Taub briefly. Jim felt his own spirits take a downward elevator ride. Research Three was not a Federal research project with security regulations to keep stockholders and other visitors at a distance. It was a private corporation, set up like many others after the Aliens had shocked Earth by landing squarely in the center of Antarctica and speaking to the world over some form of transmission which pre-empted every radio or television circuit operating at the time.

Jim had been only seven then, but he remembered the newspaper headlines. The Aliens had broken the news to Earth that there was a Federation of intelligent races out among the stars. Earth, they said, would not be allowed to send its people any further into space until the human race qualified for membership in that Federation. To qualify, humans had to develop a means of driving spaceships faster than the speed of light.

This was no small order. According to the physics developed by Albert Einstein, the speed of light represented the greatest velocity possible in the universe, roughly one hundred eighty-six thousand miles per second. But even at that speed, interstellar distances were so great that it would take three or four years to reach Alpha Centauri, the nearest worthwhile star to Earth. To reach the center of the galaxy would take twenty-five to thirty thousand years. But the Aliens, apparently, could make that trip in a few days at most. Earth must learn how to do likewise. A towering scientific problem—but how could the difficulties involved be explained to visitors at Research Three who thought Antarctica was a long way off?

"I'll get busy right away," said Jim, guiltily. "First—what?"

"One of the tiger sharks, I think—Old Susy," answered Taub. "Shunt her into the main pool here." He waved a hand at the fifty by twenty feet of four-foot-deep tank alongside him, with the massive, camera-eyed shape of the time-gap transmitter straddling it on arching steel legs. "Maybe we can get through the sharks and down to the turtles, or something else harmless by the time the visitors show up. If I'm asked one more time why we don't have muzzles on the sharks, or whether the octopi eat people, I'll quit and take a teaching job."

He looked at the time-gap transmitter, hanging over the center of the pool.

"Well, off to the salt mines," he said, beginning to climb up the ladder mounted to one of the legs of the transmitter. "Maybe we can get through in time. Get her moving, Jim."

Jim went to the tanks that held the fish and water animals. He cornered Old Susy with one of the shark tank's movable partitions, and shunted her into the water corridor leading to the experimental tank. After that it was a matter of merely herding her down the corridor and into the tank itself by sliding a partition along behind her. Used to this process as she was, Susy hardly waited to be urged. She was called Old Susy not because she was old—though at a length of twelve feet she was respectably grown up as tiger sharks went—but because she had been around longer than any other of the sharks they were using as experimental subjects.

Susy swam out into the main tank and began to cruise around after the fashion of sharks who—lacking the swim bladder of ordinary fishes—have to keep moving to keep from sinking. Taub rolled the transmitter back and forth over its tracks on either side of the pool, occasionally transmitting an impulse of timelessness of constantly varying duration into Susy's tiny "Y"-shaped brain.

Jim left the poolside to go about his main work of cleaning the tanks and cages, feeding and checking over the experimental animals—which ranged from sharks to spider monkeys. But it was a day of troubles. He was just beginning to drain and hose down the glass walls of the turtle cage, when he heard Taub calling him.

"Jim!—Jim! Hey! Get over here! I need you!"

Hastily, Jim shut off the hose, dropped it, and sprinted back to the pool. Taub was hanging so far out of his saddle behind the transmitter that it looked as if he was about to dive into the pool himself. Down below him, Susy was lying still and dead-looking, on her side on the bottom of the pool with her gills motionless.

"Slammed her with one!" shouted Taub to Jim. "Since we were late, I started her out at the top of the scale."

Reaching the poolside, Jim nodded and dove in. A couple of strokes brought him alongside the sunken shark. He got to his feet, reached down and put his arms around the sandpaper-rough body just back of the high first dorsal fin, sticking up like a sail from the spine of the shark. He lifted the tiger-striped body, righting it in the water, and began to slowly slosh with it along the length of the tank.

Susy's undershot mouth, with its murderous multiple rows of teeth, hung open and her gills stirred, opening, as the pressure of the water flowing in through the mouth and out through the gill openings pushed them. For a moment they fluttered slightly, as if Susy herself was trying to use them, then they relaxed again. Jim kept pushing the shark forward, until he came to the end of the tank, when he turned about and headed back in the opposite direction.

"How is she?" It was Taub, down from the transmitter and squatting beside the pool to hand Jim a belt with weights on it. Jim paused to hook the belt around his waist, so the weights would hold him down and give his feet traction against the bottom of the pool.

"Her gills fluttered," Jim said. "She ought to come out all right."

"Good," said Taub. "Keep walking her. That setting on the transmitter must be something special. When she comes to, I want to try her again. I've never seen one of the sharks knocked out like that before." He went back to the transmitter.

Jim kept at the necessary work of pushing Susy through the water. Without the movement-forced flow of oxygen-bearing water over and past her gills, the unconscious shark would literally drown. Coming up to one end of the pool, Jim caught sight of the milky reflection of his own image, cast back by the shadowed tile above the water at that end.

His square shoulders were hunched forward like a fullback's. Under the dark cap of his black hair and equally dark eyebrows, reflected in the tank wall, his square face was set, jaw thrust forward, almost scowling with the effort of walking the big shark's body through the water. That, he thought, as he made the turn and left the reflection behind him, was probably the way he looked to people most of the time. But he couldn't help it. Some people could do things easily, without looking as if they were working at it. He couldn't, and there was no use wishing he could. So, he told himself, heading back up toward the other end of the pool, forget it.

He did. He was good at shutting things out when he wanted to concentrate. Susy was slow coming out of her state of shock. It had always been a strange thing to Jim that a shark should give up so easily under certain conditions. The same shark that would

bite the leg off a fisherman after lying apparently
dead in the bottom of a boat, out of the water for half
an hour, was just as likely, after being carefully
netted, tanked, and carried ashore unmarked by human captors, to turn belly up and try to give up the
ghost without a struggle.

But it was this tendency to go into a sort of fatal
shock that made the shark so valuable in Taub's end
of the research, thought Jim. The sharks were far the
most sensitive to no-time, followed by the other selachians, then amphibians, and then the land reptiles.
For some reason the warm-blooded land animals were
practically immune. That should mean that humans
would also be immune to any no-time reaction—but
no one was going to risk human lives on that suppo-
sition alone. Once it was understood why contact
with an infinitesimal moment of timelessness should
send sharks into profound shock, then work on the
no-time drive could go forward . . .

Susy stirred suddenly, rasping Jim's side with the
dermal denticles, which, like small teeth rather than
scales, studded her skin.

"Coming out of it at last, are you?" grunted Jim.
None of the sharks had ever taken this long before to
recover. Perhaps . . .

"*Young man!*" screamed a strange woman's voice
somewhere above Jim. "Young man, what are you
doing down there? Answer me!"

Jim's heart sank. The visitors had evidently arrived. Well, he thought, keeping his head down and

plowing on, Taub would have to handle whoever it
was.

"Young man!" cried the voice. "Jason! Jason,
where are you? Jason—"

Jason Wells was the head of the crew on the
project. It was his unhappy duty to guide the visitors
around—when he could not find someone else to take
his place. Jason should be with this visitor, whoever
she was. And if not Jason, where was Taub, wondered Jim, making a turn at the end of the tank? But
just then he heard Taub's voice—painfully polite and
plainly unhappy.

"Jason had to go back to the office to take a
telephone call. Can I help you?"

"What's that young man doing in that water with
that shark? Doesn't he know that's dangerous? Get
him out, immediately! Get him out, I say!"

"It's not dangerous—" Taub began soothingly.

"Not dangerous! Playing with a shark big enough
to eat him alive! Don't tell *me* it's not dangerous!"

"Not," said Taub, a trifle grimly, "in this case,
ma'am. That shark you see there is stunned. Jim is
just walking her until she comes out of it. It's standard procedure."

"That's no excuse. He shouldn't have stunned her
in the first place."

"He didn't," said Taub's voice, grimly. "I did."

"You did. Why? Do you call this working on a
faster-than-light drive, young man, whoever you are—I
don't know your name."

"Taub Widerman," said Taub. "Yes, I do."

"No wonder the operating expenses of this laboratory are scandalous. Well, don't just stand there, explain yourself. What if that shark comes to and bites him?"

"When the shark comes to," said Taub's voice patiently, "she won't feel like biting anyone for some time. Just like a human being who's been knocked out, she'll be groggy for a matter of minutes and just want to be left alone. Jim, down there, will have all the time he needs to let go of her and climb out of the pool . . ."

His voice went on, explaining. Jim looked at Susy. She seemed slower than usual in coming back to consciousness. He found himself wondering what the setting had been on the transmitter, to have knocked her out so thoroughly. By watching and listening this last month that he had been working here, he had learned more than a little about how the transmitter operated. And of course the basic principle behind it had been in his high-school physics textbook . . .

He became aware that Taub, just above him, had finally got the verbal upper hand and was launched into that principle as part of the regular explanation he gave to visitors.

". . . It's all based," he was saying, "on the Uncertainty Principle stated by Werner Heisenberg in 1927. This is a fundamental statement in quantum mechanics—"

"I suppose you think I don't understand a word

you're telling me!'' interrupted the visitor's voice. "Well, you're wrong! I had college physics thirty years ago, before these modern teaching devices were around and we really had to study. I know the Heisenberg Principle. It says you can tell how fast something's moving, or where it is—but the more correct you are at telling one thing, the less correct you are about the other!''

"Er . . . yes," said Taub. "But strictly speaking, the Principle states that it's impossible to specify or determine simultaneously both the position and velocity of a particle as accurately as is wished; because the greater the precision is in one, the greater the inevitable lack of definiteness is in the other. Based on this Principle, we've evolved what we call the Theory of No-Time, which says, essentially, that if we have temporal space, or moment, so small that time does not enter the position-velocity relationship of Heisenberg's Principle, then in that moment a particle in it becomes ubiquitous—mathematically, it exists everywhere in the universe at once . . .''

Scowling at Susy's slowness to recover, Jim doggedly shoved the shark's body along.

". . . but by so-called 'gap' transmission of electronic pulses," Taub was continuing—apparently the young physicist was too involved with his visitor to notice what was happening with Susy, "at extremely high velocity, we find we can produce the impulses. It's as if you crowded together a series of waves coming in on a beach, with the result that a wave hollow was produced that went right down to the sand—so that behind the crowd of waves, there was a little strip of no water at all, moving ashore.''

Should he interrupt Taub and call his attention to the way Susy was failing to react? wondered Jim. Better wait a minute or two and see if she didn't revive naturally, after all.

"This gap we can produce seems to act the way a small segment of our theoretical no-time should act. During it, the position of a given subatomic particle becomes ubiquitous; and, theoretically at least, we can control its position when it comes out of no-time so that we can move it instantaneously from one position to another.''

Suddenly Susy twitched and shivered in Jim's arms. He looked at her hopefully.

"So our present problem," wound up Taub, "is to do the same thing with a *mass* of particles, to move a sealed vessel and its contents, like a spaceship—or a human being—''

"Then why don't you try a spaceship, instead of wasting your time playing with these sharks? I should think, young man—''

"Jim!" called another man's voice. "Jim—Taub, where's—oh, there you are, Jim!''

Jim looked up to see Jason Wells approaching the side of the tank. A tall, slim man, he came up to the edge of the tank past Taub and an enormously fat woman in a green dress—the visitor, obviously—and squatted down at the edge of the tank.

"Come here a minute, Jim," he said.

Susy was moving her gills now, even if the rhythm of their movement was somewhat ragged. Jim let her go and the shark, listing slightly to the right, swam slowly off toward the far end of the tank. Jim turned and started to slosh over to the side where Jason waited. There was an unusual touch of color in Jason's normally pale, calm face.

"Jason!" said the visitor. "Where have you been? This young man, Taub, or whatever his name is—"

"Just a minute, Mrs. Pohock," interrupted Jason without turning his head. "I've got a rather urgent message for Jim, here. Jim, your father just called."

Jim had just laid his hands on the edge of the tank, ready to hoist himself over. But at these words, he stopped in surprise.

"My dad called?" he said. "Why?"

"He wants you to come home right away," answered Jason. The unusual color over Jason's cheekbones seemed to darken and spread. Jim felt a sudden, unreasonable twinge of alarm.

"What is it?" demanded Jim, quickly hoisting himself out of the tank. He stood up, dripping, to face the tall laboratory head. "Why does he want me home right away?"

"There's a man from the federal government, from Washington, there to see you," said Jason. "And . . ." he hesitated, glancing at Taub and the visitor . . . "somebody else."

"Somebody else?" Jim stared. "Didn't he say who?"

"Yes." The color was still on Jason's cheekbones, but his voice was calm. "As a matter of fact, he did. The other . . . person . . . is the real reason both of them are there to see you. The other's an Alien."

He stood looking at Jim without moving, and Jim felt the eyes of Taub and the visitor also staring at him. Suddenly it seemed to him as if their eyes were the eyes of all the world, fastened upon him.

2

"An Alien!" echoed Jim.

Behind Jason, he could see Taub and the woman visitor gazing fixedly at him. In a world that never stopped thinking about the Aliens—but a world, also, in which few human beings had ever seen one—the words Jason had just spoken were like a summons to a royal audience, back in the days of tyrants and kings. There was something different now, Jim saw, in the faces of the three looking at him. They were watching him as strangely as if he had suddenly become an Alien himself.

"Well . . ." said Jim, awkwardly, "I guess I better get changed and start home."

"Yes," replied Jason, "you'd better not waste any time." The touches of color were fading from his cheeks, and he was observing Jim now with the coolly speculative look with which he usually studied the results of test work done by Taub and the others at the lab.

"I'll give you a call, Taub," said Jim, looking past Jason to the younger physicist, "as soon as I know what's up."

"No hurry—when you get the chance," answered Taub hastily; but Jim felt Taub and the others still watching after him as he turned and hurried off.

Twenty minutes later, dressed, he wheeled from the side road onto the cycleway and worked his way over to the far left, into the hundred-miles-per-hour-plus lane. Luckily, at this time of the day the cycleway was not crowded. With the development of electronic road-safety controls along with the gyrostabilizer, out of the gyrocontrol system that had been the ruin of Jim's own father, anyone from nine to ninety could safely ride a motorcycle. This situation, added to the development of the cycleways, with their air-curtain weather shields, could fill the lanes during the morning and evening rush hours.

Now, however, at nearly midday, the lanes were almost clear. By using the hundred-plus lane, Jim could be home in fifteen minutes. Wheeling along it, he remembered again how Jason, Taub, and the visitor had stared at him, and the back of his neck crawled with embarrassment. Of course they, like everyone else, knew about the tests to pick the Space Winners—as the news services in the continental

United States had come to call the three to be chosen
from that area. Naturally they had jumped to the
conclusion that this call from Jim's father meant that
Jim was one of the chosen, which was ridiculous, of
course.

But Jim felt an unexpected hollowness inside him.
What other reason, actually, could there be for a real,
live Alien to be at the Rawlins' home now, waiting
for him? For the first time the fact that he might
actually have been chosen became real for Jim.

It couldn't be true that he, of all people—but what
if it was?

The hollowness grew worse inside him. Now cut it
out, he told himself. Weren't you the one who kept
telling Ward Stuyler there was nothing impossible
about being picked?

Sure, answered the hollow feeling inside him. But
I didn't really believe it could happen to me. I never
actually thought I'd have to face up to whether I'd
go, or not.

But I thought you had all that settled, he argued
with himself. Didn't you make up your mind long
ago? You're no Uncle Kevin, to go haring off on
some wild deal and mess everybody up. Haven't you
had your plans made for two years, now? Start at the
University in the fall and hang on to your job part-
time at Research Three. Six years from now you'll
have your degree, and you can start working for
Research Three or some outfit like it. Any good
company will give you time off to get your advanced

degrees; and ten years from now you ought to be able to get any research job you want, doing the kind of work you want to do.

All right, that's still the sensible thing to do, isn't it? He challenged himself, swooping around one of the breathtaking curves of the cycleway as absent-mindedly as if he were riding in a bus down a city street. Nothing about the plan's changed, just because some Alien's seen fit to come calling at the house. Haven't you always told yourself you had to make up for not being clever like Enid and Terry and the folks by being clear-headed and sensible? Do you want to be another Kevin and wreck things for people? Well, do you?

No, said the hollow feeling inside him. No. But I never expected to have to make a choice like this.

Jim wheeled on around the curves of the cycleway, arguing it out with himself in the brilliant June sunlight. It was crazy to think of going off to some Alien world. His mother and father would be against it. If he considered going, they would be correct in thinking he was his Uncle Kevin all over again. But what was right?

He had told himself until now that people the age of his father and mother had simply been too old to adjust to the landing of the Aliens. The right way to deal with the Aliens, Jim and his friends all agreed, was to treat them as a fact of life. To take for granted the fact that they were there and knew more about some things than humans did—and would not tell us until we had a faster-than-light drive. Accept the facts and go ahead and make your own life.

It was a way that had seemed to work for Jim until an hour ago.

Why did I take the test anyway? Jim thought bleakly. None of us had to, they told us that at school.

But almost everyone in his high-school graduating class *had* taken it. The exceptions had been only the nuts and the oddballs. Kids who claimed to be Neo-Taylorites, wore yellow robes out of school hours and refused to think about anything unpleasant. And another, smaller bunch, who wore ancient costumes in their spare time and called themselves Archaists. These last were a crew who wanted to return to living in the Middle Ages, just as soon as they had attacked and conquered the whole Alien Federation. Most of the members of these two cults, that had sprung up since the Alien landing, were adults. But a fair number were no more than Jim's age.

They were the ones who could not learn to live with the fact of the Aliens' existence in the way Jim and his friends believed they had learned. Oh, the cultists had lots of seemingly sound arguments. Even today, crops failed for lack of weather or soil control that Alien devices could probably have provided. People died of diseases that Alien medicines almost undoubtedly could have cured—and that could be hard, to see someone in your family die, and think that the Aliens could have saved him or her, if they had wanted to do so.

But the main problem for the Neo-Taylorites and the Archaists was the crushing blow to their notions of human superiority, which the Aliens had dealt merely by revealing their existence.

What was the point of trying, asked many people, particularly those the age of Jim's father, if you knew the best you could do had already been far outdone and that what you might wear yourself out to invent had already been discovered and put to work elsewhere?

His father, like the rest, thought Jim now, grimly, would have hated the Aliens if there had been anything to be gained by hate. But there wasn't. Dogs might as well have tried to hate the race of men. The Aliens blocked the humans' road to their own future, and there was no way the humans could go forward, except on Alien terms. The older generation, particularly, had been crushed by this fact.

His generation, thought Jim, growing up in a world that knew about the Aliens, had not been crushed. But it could be, he thought now, for the first time, that his generation could possibly have stood a little crushing. It might be that those his age were trying a little too hard to turn their backs on the Aliens and pretend that the fact they were there wasn't important. It was the first time Jim had ever had that thought.

He was almost to the turnoff onto the cycleway to Northfield, where the Rawlins home was. He throttled back on the motorbike, drifted to his right through

the lanes of lesser speeds, and turned off at last on
the downward-spiraling ramp that led to the Cheshire
Hills suburb of the Northfield area. Three minutes
later, he was wheeling into the carport beside the oil
can on which Ward had perched to argue the night
before.

Both the family cars were home, plus the motorbikes of his younger sister and brother. Behind these
was a turret-top four-seater painted an official olive
drab. Jim went through the garage entrance into the
house, then through the kitchen area, around the
corner of a light-and-sound screen, into the living
room.

"Oh, there you are, Jim," said his father.

He was sitting upright in his favorite chair with the
professional look of good manners on his face. But
that face was grayer and thinner than Jim had seen it
at any time since the news of Kevin's death.

"Here are two people who've been waiting to see
you," his father went on. "Pardon me for not getting
up to introduce you gentlemen, but this heart of
mine is supposed to be coddled as much as possible."

The two men had risen to their feet as Jim came
in. Jim stared at them, for both looked like perfectly
ordinary humans in business suits, with no indication
of anything Alien about either one of them. Beyond
them, Jim saw that his whole family was present. His
mother sat in a chair beside his father's; and across
the room from his parents, on the couch, sat his sister

Enid, who was fifteen, and his younger brother, Terry, who was fourteen.

"Jim," his father was saying, "this"—he indicated the man standing closest to him—"is Mr. Walter McCreavy of the State Department in Washington. This is my son Jim, Mr. McCreavy."

Jim went forward and McCreavy, who was a slim, pleasant-looking man in his forties—about the age of Jim's father, probably, but looking much younger— shook hands with him.

Jim looked closely at McCreavy for some sign of the surprise he was used to seeing in people who had met the two younger children of the family before they met him. Enid and Terry were plainly the children of their slim, clever-looking parents. But Jim was as different as could be imagined—the younger image of his black-haired, thick-shouldered Uncle Kevin, who had made and lost three small fortunes before a fatal crash in his own light plane not only brought to ruin his final venture, but nearly did as much for Jim's family as well.

Kevin had been setting up a corporation to manufacture a revolutionary new gyrocontrol system for rockets of the U.S. Space Program, when the Aliens had landed in Antarctica. The Aliens' landing had put an end to that program and to the hopes of Kevin's corporation as well. One month later, Kevin had piloted his own light plane to a bad landing off the runway of a small-town airport in a heavy fog. The crash in which he died had revealed his corporation to consist of ten percent financing and ninety percent promises.

For months afterwards, angry or tragic-faced creditors were trying to collect from other members of the Rawlins family who had made the mistake of being involved in the corporation. Jim's dad, being the lawyer for the family, had felt himself personally responsible. He had suffered not only the expense of his services over a period of several years, helping out other members of the family and cleaning up the mess, but his own reputation as a lawyer had been damaged by popular opinion about his involvement, though actually he had been the only family member not involved in the corporation.

Where Kevin had been strong, Jim's father had always been frail, with a rheumatic heart following a bout with the fever in boyhood. The combined troubles stemming from Kevin's death and the corporation had whittled him down to a semi-invalid state. He had gotten his reputation and the family income back to normal, but his poor health and the worldwide emotional depression following the Alien landing had left him drained and cautious, even fearful. Though he never said anything, Jim knew his father worried about Jim following in Kevin's footsteps and the whole family had picked up the habit of worrying about Jim.

Only I'm not like Kevin, thought Jim. But in many ways, he knew he was. When Kevin and Jim's father had been boys together, Jim's father had been spoken of by their parents as "the clever one." Kevin had been a bull, succeeding by sheer force and drive and hard work where Jim's father used only his wits. Jim's father was still the clever one, as were Jim's mother and Enid and Terry. But Jim could not believe there was any cleverness in himself. Not the way the rest of the family, even young Terry, were always looking out for him, and stepping into situations to take care of him, whether or not he wanted them to.

Ironically, the gyrocontrol patent that was the basis of Kevin's corporation had later been bought up by a company that produced from it the gyrostabilizer for motorbikes like Jim's. This outfit had gone on to make a billion-dollar business out of the device.

But now Jim found himself shaking hands with McCreavy and the State Department man's attitude was polite enough.

"It's a real pleasure to meet you, Jim," McCreavy was saying. He had a deep, pleasant voice, at odds with his slimness. "I'd like you to meet Mr. Smith. He's a representative of the Alien Federation."

Jim turned and blinked. He found himself shaking hands with the other ordinary-looking man in a plain, gray business suit, who seemed to be about thirty years old.

"I thought you'd be an Alien . . ." he began, and then could have bitten his tongue off, for blurting it out like that. Terry would have handled it better, to say nothing of any of the rest of the family. But Mr. Smith did not seem disturbed. He smiled.

"He is," answered McCreavy.

Jim let go of the hand he was shaking with a sudden sense of shock.

"But . . ." he said; realized he was about to put his foot in his mouth again, said to heck with it, and plowed ahead. "Do you look like this usually? I mean, is this the way you actually look?"

Jim's father laughed, moving smoothly into the conversation the way everyone in the family always did to rescue Jim when he blundered.

"Yes, Mr. Smith," Mr. Rawlins said, "I didn't have the courage to ask you myself, but since Jim's brought it up—*is* this your normal appearance?"

Jim's father was not an ungifted lawyer and the professional, pleasant tones of his voice turned the conversation and the question into something casual and relaxed.

"Well," said Mr. Smith, turning to Jim's father, "that's not really an easy question to answer, in terms that would be meaningful to you. Suppose I say it's *one* of my normal appearances."

"Why don't you all sit down again?" said Mr. Rawlins. The visitors reseated themselves, and Jim found a chair opposite them that had apparently been left vacant for him, since the rest of the family were all seated a little back from it.

"I suppose you've guessed why we're here, Jim,"

said McCreavy. "You took the Alien Education Tests along with the other high-school seniors."

"But I didn't ever think I'd be picked," said Jim, bluntly. "Have I?"

"Yes," said McCreavy. "You have. You and another young man from Augusta, Maine, named Curt Harrington, and a young lady named Ellen Bouvier, from Taos, New Mexico, are the ones who qualified from the continental U.S. test area." He looked oddly at Jim. "But your father tells us you've said several times that even if you won, you wouldn't want to go. Is that the way you still feel?"

"I think so," said Jim, clumsily. He had not expected to be called on to announce his decision so quickly. "I made plans to go on to the state university, up in Minneapolis, and take a six-year physics major. I've already got a summer job with Research Three—that's one of the outfits working on the space drive—I had my plans all made," he ended up repeating lamely.

"But certainly," said McCreavy, leaning forward and staring at him, "you've got to realize that the chance to go out to the Federation worlds to study—a chance like that, that's being offered only to three out of the millions who took the test at the same time you did here in the U.S., and that'll end up being offered to only twenty young people in the whole world— you must realize how much more something like that could mean to you, compared even to the best university education you could get here on Earth?"

A little behind and off to one side of Jim, Jim's father cleared his throat.

"His going would be voluntary, I understand," said Mr. Rawlins.

"Of course." McCreavy looked past Jim at Jim's father. "The Federation tells us they wouldn't want anyone who didn't want to take advantage of their offer. Frankly, if it had been up to us, the government would have drafted the chosen ones, if we had to amend the Constitution in order to get a bill through Congress authorizing the draft."

"Any such law you got would still have to be tested in the courts before you could force anyone like Jim to go," said Mr. Rawlins.

"Yes," said McCreavy. "However, as I say, the question doesn't come up. Because the Federation wants these people only on a free, volunteer basis."

"But you won't even tell them where they're going to go or what they're going to be studying," put in Jim's mother. "How can you expect them to volunteer to go into no-one-here-knows-what?"

McCreavy looked at Smith, who picked up the conversation.

"You must believe me, Mrs. Rawlins," said Smith. "I'd be only too glad to tell you, if you had the necessary knowledge to interpret what I said in meaningful terms. But any description or explanation I gave, you'd have to interpret according to what you know of things here on Earth. Suppose I ask you a question. Suppose I said I wanted to take Jim to a place where there were areas enclosing inflammable gas mixtures, areas where temperatures of thousands of degrees were usual, and small walkways ran close to actual small rivers of molten metal? But that I told you not to worry—it'd be perfectly safe for Jim?''

''I wouldn't believe you!'' Jim's mother clasped her hands together.

Smith sat back in his chair.

''But you see,'' he said gently, ''what I've just given you is a brief description of a fully automated blast furnace, here on your own world. Do you mean to say you'd object if Jim were going on a tour of a steel plant in Pittsburgh? You see,'' he added, as Jim's mother sat rigid and silent, ''to judge the dangers of a place you've got to understand that place. Not just have a factual description of its conditions listed off for you.''

Jim's mother still said nothing. Her slim face was pale.

''But there's always danger,'' said Jim's father. ''A degree of danger's in anything. How much of a degree of danger for Jim would there be where he'd be going if he accepts? Shouldn't you be able to compare it to some equivalent situation here on Earth? For example, would it be as dangerous as going on an Arctic expedition?''

''It would and it wouldn't,'' said Mr. Smith, smiling. ''But I think I know what you mean. Suppose I say that the amount of risk Jim would be facing would be roughly equivalent to his going into military training and service in a peacetime army. In both cases he'd be away from home, largely on his own, and exposed to situations where, if he wanted to be foolhardy, he could risk bodily damage—even death. In the army, Jim could shoot himself by fooling around with his own rifle. Out among the stars he could run into equal trouble as a result of being equally irresponsible. But we know Jim pretty well as a result of the tests, and we don't think he'd be that kind of fool. Do you?''

During all this discussion, Jim had been slowly warming up under his collar.

"Then you mean—" Mr. Rawlins was beginning, when Jim interrupted.

"Just a minute, Dad."

His father looked at him with some surprise and sat back in his chair.

"Excuse me, Dad," said Jim, aware that there was a stubborn, Kevin-like note creeping into his voice, but unable to keep it out. "But everybody else seems to be trying to settle this for me. Only it's my choice, isn't it?"

Mr. Rawlins stared back at him for a second.

"We're only trying to help you, Jim," he said gently.

"But it *is* my decision? Mine to make by myself?"

"Well . . ." his father hesitated. "Legally, you know, you're still a minor . . ." He turned to look at Jim's mother, but she only looked back at him without a word. He sighed. "All right, Jim. Yes, the decision ought to be yours to make for yourself. But for what it's worth,'' he added swiftly, ''I think you ought to know that your mother and I are both against it.'' He reached out his hand to his wife and Jim's mother took it in both of hers and held it in her lap.

''It's not just that we're afraid for you, son,'' he said. ''But you had a good, sensible future all mapped out for yourself. You don't want to throw that away on some . . .'' he hesitated, ''wild venture.''

Jim felt bitter inside. He understood his father perfectly, and he saw the ghost of Kevin rising again to haunt him. His family loved him and admired him and wanted the best for him. But they all—even down to young Terry—wanted to take care of him, as if he couldn't be trusted to take care of himself.

''All right,'' Jim said. He turned to face McCreavy and Mr. Smith. ''I just wanted to make it clear that I wasn't going to be talked into anything on this— either way. Now, I'm going to ask a question. I took your tests, even if I didn't understand them. Most of the statements I had to choose yes or no on didn't make much sense to me, or else they appeared so obvious it seemed you'd have to be slightly crazy to choose any way but one. But I suppose it was a test to give you a sort of personality profile of my character. Something like the Revised Minnesota Multiphasic?''

''Yes, Mr. Rawlins,'' said the Alien, speaking directly to Jim for the first time since Jim had come into the room. ''That's correct.''

Mr. Smith's use of Jim's last name where every-one else—even McCreavy—had used his first name, plus a certain difference in the Alien's voice as he said it, sent a strange kind of shock through the air of the room. It jarred them all. But most of all, it jarred Jim.

In Smith's voice there had been a tone of respect which had not been there in his speaking to anyone else present.

It was obviously as unexpected to McCreavy as it was to Jim's family. Jim saw the State Department man staring at the Alien. McCreavy's face looked caught off guard and a little pale. It came to Jim in a sudden flash of understanding, and Jim did not ordi-narily think of himself as understanding, that McCreavy might never have heard that tone used by Mr. Smith to any other human before.

For a moment Jim's determination wobbled. Then, as he had grown into the habit of doing whenever he ran into something unexpected, he put his head down mentally and plowed onward.

"All right," Jim said, "then you must know me pretty well. Is that right?"

Mr. Smith nodded. His eyes remained steady on Jim's.

"If that's so," said Jim, plowing on, "then you must know that when I took that test I didn't have any intention of leaving Earth. I never really thought I'd be picked. But if I were picked, I had no idea of going."

"Yes, that could be seen in the results of your test," said Mr. Smith.

"All right," said Jim, unhappily aware that his jaw must be set pugnaciously, "I feel pretty good about being one of the three that were picked. And I'm not staying behind just to bask in the glory of being picked without taking any of the chances of going, or anything like that. It's just that I didn't want to go in the first place, and so I think I'm better off staying here and you're better off out there among the stars without me. Now," Jim took a deep breath, looked around the room at his silent family and then back at Mr. Smith. "I think that ought to settle it."

The Alien stood up immediately. McCreavy, left without much choice in the matter, stood up as well. Jim got up himself.

"It's your decision, Mr. Rawlins," said Mr. Smith. "The ship that is to carry the first three qualified volunteers leaves at noon tomorrow and we'd planned to give you overnight to think about it if you wished; but if you've made up your mind, I'll take it the matter is settled now."

"Good," said Jim. On sudden impulse he held out his hand and the Alien took it. "Thanks anyway. And give my best wishes to the alternate, whoever he is, who goes in my place."

"I'd be glad to," he said, "but there is no alternate."

Jim stared at the Alien.

"No alternate?" he asked.

Mr. Smith shook his head.

"Our preliminary estimate was that out of the three million young people taking the tests here in the United States, three would qualify. Believe me, we would have been happy if the entire three million could have qualified. But our estimates are usually accurate. Only three did qualify. Without you, and assuming that the other two both go, the first ship taking you human students to the stars will take off tomorrow with just those two."

He paused and looked for a moment without speaking at Jim.

"Goodbye," he said, and the odd note of respect was still there in his voice. "I'm sorry you aren't going, Mr. Rawlins, but it's been a pleasure meeting you."

The Alien turned and walked toward the door. McCreavy looked at Jim, hesitated for a moment as if he would say something, then turned and followed. They went out through the hall, and the Rawlins family in the living room heard the front door close behind the visitors.

Jim turned to look at his parents, his brother and sister. They gazed back at him without a word.

"Jim—" began his mother, sympathetically.

"No!" Jim said suddenly. "No—" He turned and went quickly through the house and out the front door. Smith and McCreavy were just at the bottom of the front steps. They turned at the sound of the front door closing behind them and halted. Jim went down the steps after them.

"I'll go," said Jim.

The Alien smiled.

"We knew you would," said Mr. Smith. "It was in the tests."

3

The olive-drab Government four-seater, carrying only Mr. Smith and the driver, was back at 7:20 the following morning in the Rawlins carport to pick Jim up and start him toward the spaceship.

Jim was grateful for this quick departure, as he had been grateful for Smith's insistence, yesterday after Jim had said he would go and the two visitors had come back into the house to discuss details of his going, that the spaceship's take-off this morning could not be delayed.

"Think of Jim's going in terms of time, rather than distance," Mr. Smith had urged the family. "It's only for the first three weeks that he'll be out of touch with you. That's a sort of probationary period. After that you can exchange letters by any spaceship of the Federation landing at Kennedy, and I believe there's one there at least twice a week. In fact, if you want to, after the first three weeks, you can board the ship and talk to Jim directly—if he happens to be someplace that has voice and picture communication equipment.''

"But if something happens . . ." Jim's mother had begun.

"If anything should happen to Jim, which is highly improbable, in our opinion," said Mr. Smith, "you'll be notified within hours, I promise you."

"What if something happens back here?" demanded Jim.

"Mr. Rawlins," said the Alien, turning to him, "we guarantee that nothing will happen back here. Since your test was checked, two weeks ago, you and your family, and the families of all those who have been chosen, have been considered exceptions to the general rule of Quarantine on Earth. Your family will continue to be under Federation protection while you are gone—and," he turned to smile at Jim's father, "that includes protection against ill health as well as any natural or human-induced disaster."

"How long," asked Jim's father, "will his course of study be?"

"That depends on a number of factors that make it impossible for us to give a precise answer at this time," answered Smith. "But I can assure you that it will not be longer than the college education he would normally be taking here on Earth."

Now, the following morning, as the Government four-seater backed out of the Rawlins driveway with Jim inside, he began to feel that perhaps he understood what the Alien had meant. The whole family, even Jim's dad, looking frail in the clear morning sunlight, was standing out in the driveway to see him off. For the first time it came to Jim, with a feeling something like a cold cramp inside him, that he might be saying goodbye to them all for good.

But the car was already backing out into the street. It turned its nose toward the distant freeway, and Jim turned his head to keep his family in sight. They were all waving. He waved back and with a powerful surge the car shot off, leaving them behind, and they were lost to sight.

Jim sat back against the soft cushions of the car's rear seat, not feeling like talking. Mr. Smith, beside him, did not press him. They rode in silence, at high speed up the police lane of the autoway, to the Navy Base adjoining the Minneapolis-St. Paul Metropolitan Airport.

The car took them right out onto the concrete pad, up beside a Navy rocket interceptor, sitting powerful and stubby, like a broad arrowhead without a shaft, aimed at a forty-five degree angle toward the blue morning sky. Jim and Mr. Smith both got out, Jim carrying a small overnight bag with a few personal belongings in it. He had been told by Smith that actually he need bring nothing, that he could step aboard the spaceship in just the clothes he was wearing, and be provided for in every way. But there were a few things like his slide rule and a notebook that he intended to hang onto until he actually came face to face with better Alien equipment.

The interceptor's pilot was already in the front seat of the two-place ship and the rocket tubes were rumbling in a warm-up undertone.

"Well," said Mr. Smith, stopping beside the handholds leading to the cockpit, "this is goodbye, Mr. Rawlins. You'll have a little walk to the spaceship after you land at the Cape, but you can't miss seeing it." He offered his hand and Jim shook it.

"But who do I see aboard the ship?" Jim asked. Now that he was being parted even from Smith, he had the last-minute empty feeling that there were a thousand more questions he should have asked and had not. "I mean, do I report to one of the ship's officers, or something?"

"I don't believe you'll meet any of the personnel of the ship," Smith said, smiling. "In fact, the ship may not have any—no, don't ask me to explain that. Just go out to the ship, and you'll be taken care of."

"But—I won't see anybody?" Jim lingered with one hand on a handhold sticking out from the bulging side of the muttering interceptor.

"You'll be meeting your fellow students," said the Alien. "Oh, and you'll be meeting one other passenger, a Federation citizen who's been on Earth a little while now and is just leaving."

"An . . ." the word seemed hardly polite, but Jim could not think of any other that fitted the matter, ". . . Alien?"

Smith's smile broadened for once, almost into a grin.

"An Atakit, to be precise," he said. "He'll no doubt tell you all about himself when you meet him. You'd better get aboard now. The pilot's waving for you to climb in."

He shook hands for a last time with Jim.

"Don't worry," he said, looking keenly at Jim. "Follow instructions when you've got them. When you haven't, use your head sensibly and everything will work out all right. The tests showed this about you."

"Thanks," said Jim. With his overnight bag dangling from one hand, he began to climb up into the cockpit.

About an hour later, he was walking across an expanse of concrete toward the Alien spaceship. It struck him that the Alien ship looked a little like a building—a miniature skyscraper with four equal sides narrowing toward the top, which had a point like a four-sided pyramid. The only difference was that the ship was black and completely without windows.

He trudged along. He was almost to the Alien spaceship now, feeling rather small and unimportant compared to the expanse of concrete and the towering ship, and as far as he could see there was no door or airlock visible in the black side facing him. He wondered for a moment if he was expected. It would be pretty embarrassing to reach the ship and simply be left, standing there, with no way to get in, and ignored.

He was now in the shadow of the ship, and still nothing had happened. A few more steps and he would be walking right into the side of it.

A sudden darkening of the concrete around him made him look up.

Some twenty feet overhead and coming down smoothly, was a platform about ten feet square, apparently unconnected with the side of the ship or anything else. Above it a large, square opening had appeared in the side of the ship about thirty feet above Jim's head. The platform landed as lightly as a puff of smoke at Jim's side.

"Please step aboard," said a voice, rather like that of Mr. Smith, out of the empty air.

Jim stepped on to the platform, walked to the center of it, and was borne aloft. The platform slid up along the side of the ship and through the opening. Behind Jim, he heard the faint sound of something like a door closing and found himself at one end of a pleasantly lighted, silent corridor with bright metal walls and ceiling and what appeared to be soft yellow carpeting underfoot. The color of the carpeting was reflected in the walls and ceiling.

"Will you walk along to the door at the end of the corridor?" said the same voice that had spoken from the platform. It sounded as if it were speaking at shoulder height in the air at Jim's side. "Through the door you will find your quarters, from which there is access to other parts of the ship."

Jim walked forward. The corridor seemed only about thirty feet long, and the metal-bright door at the end swung open as he approached it. He stepped through the doorway into a room very much like the bedroom of a hotel suite on Earth, except that there were no windows.

He laid his overnight bag on the luggage rack and went through a further doorway into what was evidently the sitting room connected with the bedroom. Here, too, it was like any hotel, but there were no windows. There was a further door, but when he took hold of its doorknob, the door would not open.

"It would be appreciated," said the voice beside him, in such a lifelike manner that he almost turned to see who was standing there, "if you would not leave your own quarters for the lounge and other areas until the ship has taken off. You are the last of the three to board, and take-off will be within a few minutes. The door to the lounge will open automatically once the ship is in interstellar space."

"All right," said Jim, and then got the feeling of foolishness that always came to him on finding he had answered a recorded message heard over the telephone at home. He left the door and went back to sit down in one of the overstuffed armchairs of the sitting room.

Beside him was a low table on which he saw several copies of American magazines. He picked up a copy of *Research Digest,* and saw that it was the latest issue. It was one of the few magazines he read regularly, but this particular issue didn't seem to have anything much worth reading in it. He got up and took another tour of his two rooms; but there was nothing to discover except that the drawers of the dresser in the bedroom turned out to be full of either his own clothes or exact imitations of them. The same situation prevailed in the closets, where most of his own wardrobe at home, or its duplicate, seemed to be hung up neatly.

An idea struck Jim—something he had intended to do as soon as he got aboard the Alien ship, and which he had forgotten. He went back to his overnight bag and got out his diary-notebook. Checking his watch, he saw that it was 10:07 A.M. He wrote this down, estimated his actual arrival time on the ship as about 10:00 even, and put down that in parentheses, with a note that it was an estimate.

Replacing the notebook in the bag, he went back to the sitting room and sat down again in the chair beside the magazines.

He wondered when the Alien ship was going to take off. The voice that had spoken to him had given him the idea that it would happen in a minute or two, but time was ticking by and apparently nothing had happened. Well, thought Jim, feeling a slight twinge of stubbornness, I'm in no rush if they aren't.

He picked up the magazine, and began to read the first article in it—something about an improved gyrostabilizer for vehicles. But as things were with him now, it didn't matter much to Jim whether they improved the gyrostabilizers on motorbikes or not. His mind wandered. Come to think of it, he thought, Mr. Smith had been pretty evasive. The truth of the matter was, Jim had no idea of what lay waiting for him at the end of this voyage.

For one thing, Jim thought now, what was he going to be studying? The interstellar civilization of the many races that made up the Alien Federation, he supposed. Sort of like a massive civics course to start off with. The government setup that kept all these peoples and worlds together, their trade and customs, and so forth. That was probably why for the first three weeks the human students wouldn't be able to get in touch with people back home. The Aliens didn't want them going off half-cocked before they'd completed their orientation course that gave them the completed picture of how it was among the stars.

But evidently the Aliens must feel pretty sure that once the human students had gone through the three-week course that they'd be pretty well sold on the Federation setup. But what if they weren't? What then? Mr. Smith hadn't said anything about dissatisfied students being able to drop out and go home, with no questions asked.

What if—the chiming of a musical note made him

look up. He saw the formerly locked door now standing open.

"The ship," said the voice he had heard before, "is in interstellar space. The lounge and related areas are now open to you."

Jim dropped his *Digest* and stared. They couldn't be in space already. As he stood up, the voice spoke again.

"Your destination will be approximately fifteen hundred light-years from your home planet. Arrival time will be in approximately four of your hours. If you should wish for anything, please speak the wish aloud. If it is possible at all to satisfy your desire with the facilities of this ship, satisfaction will be attempted. To order food and drink in the dining area, simply give your order aloud and be prepared for a wait of not more than five minutes for delivery of what you have ordered."

The voice stopped. Jim started up again. He walked ahead, through the open door, and down another of the softly bright corridors to step into a further room.

Quite plainly, this was the lounge. It was a wide, carpeted room about the size of his sitting and bed-room together at the other end of the connecting corridor. Comfortable chairs and couches were scattered around it, and there was an opening to Jim's left through which he could see a smaller room set with dining tables and chairs. In the lounge proper, he saw two other doors, one open and one closed.

To Jim's right the wall was blank, but straight

ahead it held a screen of some sort that must be easily five feet on a side. Pictured on the screen right now was a panorama of stars in the variety of colors that can be observed only in airless space. Jim blinked. The fact that they could get off Earth and into inter-stellar space in minutes without his even feeling the take-off had been wild enough. Now the screen was evidently showing the stars as the ship moved past them at a speed many times that of light toward their fifteen-hundred-light-years' distant destination.

"They can't do that!" said Jim out loud.

A large armchair with its back to Jim, facing the screen, suddenly produced the top of a small, blonde head. The next second, a girl, looking not much older than Jim's fifteen-year-old sister, Enid, stuck her face around the side of the chair to look at him.

Jim blinked. Someone that young? Another of the Space Winners?

"What can't they do?" asked the girl.

"That!" growled Jim, pointing at the screen and coming forward. "At speeds faster than light the screen shouldn't look like that—and we've got to be doing faster than light to get where we're going, fifteen hundred light-years in four hours! We ought to be leaving behind us the light of the stars we've passed so that it'd be dark there, and the stars ahead would be streaks—" He broke off, not exactly sure how it would be, at that.

"Maybe they've adjusted it somehow," said the

girl. "Anyway, it worked all right when the ship took off."

Jim gazed at her, sitting in the big chair. She was small, rather friendly looking, but nothing to write home about in the beauty department. She looked two or three years too young to be a high-school senior, let alone a graduate.

"You're Ellen Bouvier?" Jim asked.

"I am," she said interestedly. "Why does that make you mad?"

"Mad?" Jim woke up to the fact that he was scowling. "I'm not . . . I mean, it's just a habit of mine." He made an effort to unkink his face.

"Well," she said, after a second, "which one are you? Curtis Harrington? Or James Rawlins?"

"Oh. Sorry," said Jim. "Jim Rawlins. You're pretty young, aren't you?"

He was instantly aware that he had blundered as usual. Ellen's small, friendly face stiffened.

"*I* don't think so," she said frostily. She stared at him for a moment, then apparently relented. "As a matter of fact," she said, "I'm just nine months and four days younger than you are."

Jim blinked.

"You are?" he said. "I mean, how do you know?"

"I asked," she said, "the Alien who told me I'd been picked by the tests. I wanted to know about the two I'd be going with. Didn't you ask?"

Jim shook his head. It had never occurred to him to ask about his fellow students. Now, however, something Ellen had said a moment before came back to his mind to bother him.

"You said," Jim said, "that you watched the ship take off from Earth—from the lounge here, watching the screen?"

"Why, yes," said Ellen. "I'd never thought I'd get the chance to watch a take-off from inside a spaceship leaving Earth. I didn't want to miss it. Didn't you know you could see it from the lounge?"

"Even if I'd known it," said Jim, "it wouldn't have made any difference. I've been locked up until just now, in my own quarters."

He sat down on a chair beside hers and stared at her. Ellen stared back.

"That's funny," said Ellen. "My door to the lounge here was open, and that voice that talks to you even suggested I might like to watch the take-off on the screen, here."

"Real funny!" growled Jim.

"Oh, well," said Ellen. "Maybe, if you know a lot about spaceships, there might be something they didn't want you to see until you'd had proper training. But since I don't know anything about it, they didn't mind my watching." She seemed to dismiss the matter lightly, but her voice was oddly thoughtful as she finished speaking.

"Only I don't," said Jim, suddenly also thoughtful.

"Don't what?" She gazed at him curiously.

"Don't know anything about spaceships—let alone Alien ones. I mean, I've had high-school physics and learned a little more on my own. Oh, and I've heard the physicists talk at Research Three about Alien ships—"

Jim broke off, caught up in his thoughts. Ellen, he realized, had not carried her explanation to its logical implications. Why should the all-powerful Aliens have anything to hide from any Earth human like himself? It struck a false note. There couldn't be something more to this business of taking young human volunteers out to the stars than the Aliens had admitted, or could there? Abruptly uneasy and a little suspicious, Jim tucked the question away in the back of his head for examination at his leisure, later.

"What's Research Three?" Ellen was asking.

"Place I had a summer job," muttered Jim. It came to him he might learn something by questioning Ellen. "Did you have any physics in school?"

"None." Ellen shook her head. "Anthropology and biology were my sciences. I'm going into sociology in college—I mean, I was."

"Sociology?" Jim caught himself scowling again and stopped himself. "That's sort of an odd basis for getting picked like this, isn't it? I mean, sociology deals with the human race, and if there's one thing we aren't going to be running into with the Aliens, it'll be Earth-type sociology."

"I suppose we're going to be dealing with Earth-type physics?" said Ellen.

"That's different," said Jim, regretfully, seeing he had stirred her up again. "Alien physics has to be a lot more advanced than ours, granted. But it almost has to use what we know about physics as a base. The same with all the hard sciences like chemistry and, say, meteorology. But a soft science like sociology where it's all guesswork—"

"Guesswork!" snapped Ellen. "I suppose you're one of those people that think—" But she was interrupted before she could begin to get properly wound up on what was obviously a sore point with her.

"All hail!" cried a voice behind them. They both jumped to their feet and turned around to see the last sort of apparition Jim had expected to encounter aboard this Alien spaceship.

Emerging from the remaining locked doorway—now open—was an astonishing young man well over six feet tall and thin as the long rapier in the scabbard banging at his heels. From high-crowned feather hat to thigh-high, soft leather boots, he was dressed in the costume of an English cavalier of the seventeenth century. Smiling widely across his long, thin face, the newcomer loped up to them and caught up Jim's right hand, shaking it energetically.

"You must be Rawlins!" he cried. "Jim Rawlins? I'm Curt Harrington. And you," he turned to Ellen, "Ellen Bouvier, right?"

He let go of Jim's hand and threw Ellen a sort of half-cheerful, half-embarrassed salute.

"Pleased to meet you both. Down with the Aliens?"

Jim stared at him. This latest arrival, he found himself thinking, was just about the final ridiculous touch on the whole crazy business.

"You're an Archaist?" he managed to ask, finally.

"Right!" cried Curt. "First, last, and always an Archaist. First, last and always a man of Earth. Did the Aliens who talked to you two tell you what I wrote on my tests at the time I took them?"

"No," said Jim, glumly, sitting down in his chair again. A Space Winner who was a Neo-Taylorite, one of the group who wanted people to stick their heads in the sand, ostrich-style, and ignore the Aliens, would have been farfetched enough. But an Archaist— one of the bunch who had dreams of building a secret fleet of human spaceships, attacking the Alien Federation and conquering it for Earth—this was beyond any kind of sense. Of all the possibilities involving the third member of their group, it was the last Jim would have imagined.

But here it was, big as life in its boots and rapier, telling Ellen all about it—since Jim had rather withdrawn from the conversation by sitting down as he had.

". . . I wrote," Curt was saying to Ellen as confidentially as was practical, considering the more than a foot of difference in height between them, " 'Down with the Aliens! If you accept me on the basis of this test, you do so at your own risk!'—And I signed it, 'Curtis Walter Harrington.' "

"Well," Ellen said, "it doesn't look as if you scared them off from choosing you."

"Scared them off? No!" said Curt. "They took up my challenge. That's why I wore my uniform aboard the ship here, to show them that I understood!" He looked over at Jim. "People back home expected me to refuse when I was chosen. Hah! Pass up the opportunity to scout the Aliens on their home worlds? Not a chance! I'll learn all I can and try to get back to Earth in one piece, against the day we rise for our freedom . . ."

Jim tried to shut off his hearing, internally. He had listened to this sort of thing before from those in his high school who wore the Archaist "uniform." A cold despair began to creep through him. He had thrown over all his plans for the future on an impulse. He had let himself be carried away by the fact that if he did not go out to the stars, the human race would lose one-third of this chance to study the sciences of the Federation's superior civilization.

Now, this was how it had turned out. He found himself teamed with a scientifically uneducated girl and a crackpot. He himself had been a strange enough choice for the Aliens to pick if they were serious about educating the best of Earth's emerging generation. After all, thought Jim glumly, he was far from being the brightest, even in his own high school. His grades had been good, but only because he dug in and slugged away at every subject until he almost knew it by heart. Nor was he particularly sharp in other departments. He was not clever at dealing with people, and things happening around him practically had to hit him like a sledgehammer before he caught on to what they meant.

So, where did that leave the Federation? With a thick-headed character like himself, a girl sociologist probably loaded down with nutty theories instead of solid facts, and a basketball-player-shaped crackpot. It just didn't add up. Something was phony about the whole setup. One unlikely human subject for special education, brooded Jim, he could have swallowed. Three, the way it had turned out, was too much for anybody to accept.

Whatever the Aliens had in mind, it could not be, as they had said it was, educating the best of Earth's young adults, so that they could come home again and lead the human race into a brighter and better future. This thing that Jim had gotten himself into was not so much a plan for Earth's betterment, it was a circus with himself as one of the three funny animals. All that was lacking was the ringmaster. Jim glowered sideways and up at Curt and Ellen, who evidently felt not the slightest touch of his suspicions, and were getting along like long-lost cousins at a family reunion.

". . . The lesson of history," Curt was saying enthusiastically, "gives us the clue to understanding the Aliens. Seen in the light of our own human history, they're exactly like the mercantile class spreading out in medieval Europe, or the Europeans moving into North America. A case of overlapping of different ethical and moral standards—''

A sound like a huge gong drowned out what he was going to say. All three of the humans jerked about and stared at the blank wall to the right of the screen. As they looked, it rang again, then split from top to bottom. The sound of a raging bass voice uttering incomprehensible syllables blasted from the crack.

''. . . *Rrrryllovarrk! Chrr kii y uppsk! Rgggt, gtt minnn! Klask . . .''*

With another explosion of torn metal, the crack ripped wide. A squirrel-like head somewhat smaller than a human's poked through the opening. The brown eyes examined the three humans, and the stiff, black whiskers below the pointed nose visibly wilted.

''Oh, my!'' said the head, tragically in English. ''Oh my, oh my, oh my! How could I?''

Whiskers quavering with emotion, the head leaned forward, two small furry hands appeared, and each grasped an edge of the crack. As the squarrel-like face winced at the further sound of tearing metal, the delicate-appearing hands ripped apart and spread the crack wide enough to step through. They did this with as little apparent effort as if the partition was constructed of ordinary note paper instead of metal.

The newcomer stepped through the hole in the wall

into their midst and looked pleadingly up at them from his three feet of height.

"Young friends!" he said, deeply and heart-rendingly, clasping his small hands together. "I have alarmed you! I have disturbed you! Once again my fearful temper, my brutish strength—so inescapable in one from a world of harsher gravity than your gentle Earth—has betrayed me!"

The three humans stared at this small, bass-voiced apparition, at a loss for words.

"Please!" boomed the small Alien, striking himself punishingly on the forehead with a sound like a sledge hammer striking an oak block. "Tell me how I can make amends. Oh, hard is the road of nonviolence for the unenlightened! When will I learn to control this vicious and brutal rage that is my birthright?"

The other three still stared, wordless. But in Jim, at least, the wordlessness was being matched by a definite feeling of unhappy realization, like a sinking sensation.

The ringmaster had arrived. The Alien before them was wrapped in the yellow robes of the Neo-Taylorite cult, sworn opponents of Archaists like Curt.

4

As the three of them stood staring, without answering, the Alien's black whiskers slowly wilted again. A bright tear welled out of one eye and trickled down his nose to drop to the carpet.

"Quite right, young friends," said the little Alien, tragically. "You're quite right! I'm not fit to be spoken to. What violence to your emotions I've committed. And I had planned it so differently. I was going to approach you politely, knocking to give warning of my entrance. I was intending to introduce myself but no more."

He broke off, his whiskers stiffening.

"Such is the just reward of uncontrolled violence!" he said, turning about. "I shall withdraw to the room from which I came and leave you to try to forget the sight of me—''

Jim opened his mouth, getting to his feet, and he, Curt, and Ellen found themselves speaking all at once.

"Hold on—" began Jim.

"Just a minute—" began Curt.

"You certainly aren't going off like that!" said Ellen, and somehow having gotten out ahead of Jim and Curt, continued while they fell silent. "You didn't do any violence to us at all. You just surprised us!"

The little Alien had swung back, brightening at her words.

"Only surprised—?" he broke off, doubtfully. "Of course, surprise is a form of violence. . . . But," he cried deeply and happily, brightening again, "if you forgive me, the damage may be mended. I am overwhelmed to make your acquaintance. You must be Ellen Bouvier?"

"That's right," said Ellen, smiling at him. "And this is Curt Harrington," she pointed to the tall figure beside her, "and Jim Rawlins."

"Honored! Honored to make the acquaintance of you all!" cried the Alien, beaming. "Let me introduce myself, an erring and faulty student of nonviolence. I am an Atakit, from Juseleminopratipup. My name is Panjarmeeklotutmrp!"

Jim, Ellen, and Curt stared at each other and back at the Alien.

"Pan . . ." began Jim, hesitantly, after a second.

"Oh, call me Peep. Call me Peep!" boomed the little Atakit, exuberantly. "All humans do. My unfortunate name is impossible for them to pronounce. Excuse it! Excuse my temper. The last thing in the universe I wished to do was shock your sensibilities by such a crude demonstration of violence, but the door of a cabinet in my quarters happened to stick, and one thing led to another. You have no idea," continued Peep, earnestly, "young friends, how the perversity of an inanimate object can try a temper like mine."

"You really have one, haven't you?" said Curt, scowling at him. "Are you really a Neo-Taylorite?"

"An imperfect disciple of that great human movement, yes," said Peep, hanging his head. "But only the last few months or so. Before that I was a typical member of the Atakit race—and you must understand, young friends," he went on, looking up at them again, "that the accident of evolution that brought us Atakits to civilization on a heavy-gravity world originally populated by many kinds of dangerous animal life has unfortunately produced a people with a high index of combativeness. We are built to fight at the drop of a hat, as you say on Earth—in fact, the slight tilting of a hat is sufficient."

He stopped talking and sighed heavily.

"And, of course," he added, "this is complicated by the fact that in a world of lesser gravity like your own, or aboard ship here where the gravity is adjusted to your comfort, the slightest loss of control can lead to truly regrettable incidents. But,'' he added, brightening once more, ''let us not talk of that. Enough that I am a student, as you are students. Shall we consider ourselves students together?''

His black nosetip lifted hopefully to them.

''Just let me ask you something,'' said Curt. ''How old are you?''

''Let me see, young friend,'' beamed Peep. ''In your Earthly terms . . . somewhat more than two hundred years old. In my terms, as life spans are measured among the Atakits, I have been adult for about the last hundred and fifty of those years.''

''Ah,'' said Curt. ''Now, if you don't mind, I want to talk something over with my friends, here. You stay where you are. We'll be right back.''

''By all means. I shall sit down on the floor here and contemplate the stars,'' said Peep, doing just that and gazing at the screen with its view of passing space. ''How beautiful they are. How . . . how shall I put it? How *intrinsically* nonviolent!''

Curt grabbed Jim and Ellen by an arm apiece and led them off down the corridor leading to his own quarters, which were an exact duplicate of Jim's.

''Listen,'' he said, in a low voice, when he had closed the door behind them, ''he's a spy!''

''Spy?'' said Ellen.

''Sure,'' said Curt, bending down to glare at them both. ''Did you ever see anything as fake as his breaking down that wall and then pretending to be a

Neo-Taylorite? As if an Alien would be caught dead
belonging to an Earth group, particularly a collection
of nuts like those Neo-Taylorites! We're supposed to
think he's completely harmless and let him tag along,
and all the time he'll be taking notes on what we do
and say and think.''

"How's he going to know what we think?'' asked
Jim. But before Curt could answer, Ellen had snatched
up the conversational ball and was running with it.

"That's ridiculous!'' she said. "If the Aliens wanted
to keep track of us, they wouldn't have to plant
somebody with us. They must have ways of doing it
with concealed microphones and equipment like that.
Besides, what're they going to learn from us that
they don't know about humans already?''

"How do we know what they don't know?'' asked
Curt. "I tell you he's a spy. I can see it with one eye
closed.''

"What you can see,'' said Ellen, "is that he's
wearing a Neo-Taylorite robe, and you don't like
Neo-Taylorites.''

"You like him,'' accused Curt. "That's your trouble.
He's already charmed you. You *like* him.''

"All right, I like him! That's as good a reason for
thinking he's not a spy as your not liking him is for
thinking he is a spy.''

"Listen—'' began Jim.

"I observe. You're just going by how you feel.
In—''

"Hold it!"

Curt and Ellen both stopped talking, stopped glaring at each other, and turned to Jim with startled expressions. It occurred to Jim that maybe he had spoken up a little more strongly than he had intended to. It was his usual problem, again. First he couldn't get a word in edgewise when an argument was going on, then when he did get people to listen, he evidently sounded as if he was about to start swinging at anyone in sight.

"I mean," said Jim, trying to smooth the hard edge of exasperation off of his voice and sound reasonable, "let's not get all worked up over something we can't prove one way or another. What if he isn't a spy? There's no way of making sure when we've just met him, is there? And what if he is?" Jim turned to Curt. "Are you going to throw him out of the lounge bodily? If you try it, don't count on my help. Did you see how he spread that crack in the metal wall?"

The tall youth and the small girl stared back at Jim without answering.

"What I'm driving at," Jim continued, "is why don't we just go back and act as polite toward him as he's acting toward us? Since we can't do anything else about it, in any case. Anyway, I'm going back. Now."

Turning on his heel, Jim headed back toward the lounge. As he went down the corridor, he heard the footsteps of the other two behind him. He emerged into the lounge once more. Peep was still sitting watching the screen.

"Peep," said Jim, advancing toward him across the carpet, "can you tell from what you see on the screen there, how far we are from Earth right now?"

Peep bounced to his feet and turned around, beaming.

"Why, yes, young friend," he replied, "roughly, of course." He glanced back for a moment at the screen. "I would guess we're approximately thirteen or fourteen hundred light-years from Earth at the present moment. And, of course—"

He did not finish.

Suddenly there was a sound as if the whole space-ship surrounding them had been pounded by a single blow from some mighty club. It rang and reverberated all around them, and suddenly there was no more gravity. Jim found himself floating off the floor with the small effort he had made to look around when the noise rang out. Ellen, Curt, and even Peep, were also drifting out of touch with the floor.

"What—" cried Ellen. But before she could finish what she was trying to say, the gravity came back on, and they all fell sprawling on the floor.

"What happened?" demanded Curt, bewilderedly, sitting up and rubbing the back of his head. Jim was already scrambling back on to his feet. He helped Ellen up, and by the time this was done, both Curt and Peep were on their feet as well.

"Yes. What was it?" asked Jim, turning on Peep. "Did something hit the ship?"

"No, no, young friend!" said Peep, distressed, pawing the air with his little hands. "Impossible. Nothing can go wrong or happen to a ship on such a flight as this. I assure you. Some minor malfunctioning of machinery is all it can be."

"It didn't sound minor to me," muttered Curt.

"But I give you my word, young friend," said Peep, turning to him. "Accidents to a ship in flight in interstellar space simply cannot take place. Oh, theoretically, something could happen. But as a practical matter, not for hundreds of thousands of your Earthly years has an accident occurred. It is im—"

The whole ship rang again. Once more gravity went off. This time the ship lurched as it sounded, and not only the humans and Peep this time, but the furniture of the lounge was floating and drifting around in mid-air.

"I assure you," Peep began once more, sounding as if he was in an agony of embarrassment, "even if the impossible should happen, safety measures have been provided—"

"Attention!" The voice that Jim had heard on his arrival aboard this ship was this time speaking much more loudly and on a note of urgency. "Attention, all passengers! This ship has been severely damaged and has become unsafe. I repeat, this ship is no longer safe for the passengers. All passengers will proceed through the corridor from the quarters of the

Atakit, Panjarmeeklotutmrp, to the ship's lifeboat, which will transport all passengers to a beaconed world. I repeat, all passengers proceed by way of the corridor from the Atakit quarters to the ship's lifeboat, which will transport you to the nearest beaconed world. To facilitate your reaching the lifeboat, gravity will be restored for fifteen minutes. Do not delay. The restoration of gravity will shorten the time before the ship becomes uninhabitable. You have fifteen minutes only to leave the ship. Repeat, fifteen minutes. Move quickly."

Gravity came back on. Once more the three humans tumbled, but Peep, evidently prepared this time, came down solidly and firmly on his feet, batting aside a sofa that attempted to contest his landing area.

Jim looked quickly at his watch. It was five minutes after twelve.

"This way, young friends," Peep said calmly. "It will be quickest by my emergency route."

He turned about and with one thrust of his arms, spread wide the rent in the metal wall through which he had entered the lounge. He stepped through and beckoned the others to follow him.

They did not waste time. Curt first, Ellen next, and Jim bringing up the rear, they stepped gingerly past the razor edges of the torn metal and into a room, which was evidently Peep's bedroom. It was designed as Jim's had been, except it lacked a dresser, and had a sort of oversized hassock instead of an Earth-style bed.

"This way," said Peep, leading the way at a trot into another room where smaller hassocks were spotted about the floor. He led them to one of three doors set close to each other.

"This is the corridor to which we have been referred," Peep said.

They followed him to the end of the corridor, and found themselves face to face with a heavy metal door.

The door was jammed.

"Mttr yssk!" muttered Peep, when it resisted him. He turned his head to look back over his shoulder. "Young friends," he said, "could I bother you to back up about halfway down the corridor?"

Jim, Ellen, and Curt backed up. Peep backed up also. Then he charged the door.

He was as fast as he was strong. One moment he was standing before them, the next there was a swoosh of movement and a slam from the end of the corridor, followed by an explosion of Atakit fury.

Suddenly there was no door there. It and Peep, too, had vanished. There was silence. The three humans looked at each other.

Jim glanced at his watch. It was twelve-fifteen.

"Come on!" he said. He led the way at a run down the corridor and through the ruins of the doorway. Beyond was a small room, its further side occupied by what was obviously the hull of some kind of spacecraft, with a round, heavy door in its side standing ajar.

"Inside!" said Jim, and led the way pell-mell into the ship. As Curt, who was last, passed the threshold, the door swung closed behind him.

"All passengers," said a voice that was in no way different from the voice they had grown accustomed to aboard the large spaceship. "All passengers take seats immediately. The lifeboat will go on independent power in twenty seconds. Take seats immediately, please!"

There were four seats that looked more like padded cups than anything else. Jim spotted Peep in one of the front pair of seats and scrambled into the cup beside him. He turned his head and saw Curt and Ellen getting into the cups behind.

The moment Jim had settled fully into the seat, a strange sensation moved over him. It was as if some invisible but heavy liquid quickly filled up the cup around him until it covered him completely, to the top of his head. He had no difficulty breathing, but if he had been suddenly immersed in mercury he could not have been more effectively cushioned and packed.

Slowly, and with difficulty, he managed to turn his head to look over the rim of his cup at Peep beside him. The Atakit was seated in his own cup, on his haunches, staring straight ahead. His face was a mask of sorrow.

"Peep!" said Jim, hearing his own voice strangely, as if he spoke underwater. "Peep, are you all right?"

The Atakit did not stir. As if from a great distance, his voice drifted back to Jim's ears. It was as sad and thin as the voice of a ghost.

"Do not speak to me, young friend," it said. "I am not fit."

"But Peep—" Jim broke off. It was plain the Atakit was no longer listening. His eyes were closed, and he sat motionless. And just then, Jim forgot all about talking to anyone. Because in the same moment, the lifeboat took off from the spaceship under its own power.

Evidently there were none of the magical devices aboard the lifeboat that the large ship had possessed, to make take-off and travel accelerations something the passengers did not even feel. The acceleration of the lifeboat must have been massive beyond human experience. Even under the protection of whatever held Jim in his cup, the pressures were like a mountain bearing down on every inch of his body. He blacked out.

When he swam groggily back up to consciousness, the feeling of being immersed in mercury was gone. The bulkhead of the lifeboat directly in front and curving back overhead to form the ceiling above all four seats had somehow turned itself into a vision screen. Sitting in his cup, Jim could see the face of a world below them, toward which the lifeboat was steadily descending.

What he saw was mainly ocean, dotted with occasional islands, some larger, some smaller, but none large enough to really dominate the others, for example, the way that the island of Hilo dominates the lesser Hawaiian Islands. The ocean between these islands was darker than the oceans on Earth—an indigo, almost a blue-black in color.

They were evidently descending at a high rate of speed toward an island with an extinct and foliage-covered, if tall, volcano somewhat off center in its midst. Just as the waters were a darker blue than the sea waters of Earth, so the local jungle or forest or whatever it was seemed to be a lighter green. This contrast made the island stand out brightly against the ocean.

"Please remain in your seats," said the voice over their heads. "For protection against the deceleration of landing, please remain in your seats."

It was obvious now that they were plunging toward the surface of the world below at a rate that would have burned up a meteor or any Earth-constructed air or spacecraft from the friction of the atmosphere against the fast-moving hull of the lifeboat. But no heat was felt inside the lifeboat, and on the screen no glow of combustion was to be seen between them and the scene below. The invisible, mercurylike substance welled up around Jim again.

He felt the pressure of deceleration, but it was not nearly the pressure he had felt when the lifeboat had left the Alien spaceship. He saw the green surface of the volcano's side leaping up toward them on the screen—and then, suddenly, with the audible sound of breaking branches heard through the lifeboat's hull, they had plunged through the roof of tree-limbs and were on the ground.

The invisible, mercury-heavy protection drained away from around Jim once more.

"You are on the Class Four Quarantined Planet of Quebahr," announced the voice overhead, clearly. "According to programming, this lifeboat has landed you at the optimum point on the planet's surface for entry concealed from the native life. As a Class Four Quarantined World, Quebahr is barred from all knowledge of the Federation, or of life beyond its atmosphere. Since leaving the spaceship you have accordingly been hypnotically conditioned against imparting that knowledge to any local peoples."

Jim stared in the direction from which the voice seemed to be coming. He did not feel hypnotically conditioned, but maybe you couldn't tell.

"The Quarantine on this world is considered to be of greater importance than the lives of any Federation people who happen to be castaway on it," went on the voice. "Consequently, while everything will be done to rescue you, all efforts in this direction are subject to the maintenance of the Quarantine. It was for this reason you were not set down next to the beacon which will summon a rescue ship, but in this most inconspicuous spot."

The voice paused.

"Mechanisms aboard this craft," it went on after a second, "will supply you with all necessary clothing, equipment, and instruction to aid you in reaching the beacon location by your own efforts and without alarming the local peoples. You have two hours, by Earth-time standard, to make use of these mechanisms.''

Once more, the voice paused.

"Two hours from the conclusion of this announcement," it said. "At the end of two hours exactly, this craft will destroy itself and anything within the radius of its own length surrounding it.''

5

". . . No, no, young friend," said Peep, sighing heavily. "You are better off without me. I am unfit. Just—leave me here and save yourselves. You, this innocent world, the universe, are all safer without my presence."

They had managed to get Peep out of his cup-seat and out of the lifeboat to a safe distance. But from that point on, he had resisted them. He sat disconsolate on the mossy ground.

"I ask myself," he went on, "was it necessary at all? Was there any need to fly into a rage simply because a door would not open? Would you do it, young friends?"

"Yes," said Curt, with sudden inspiration. "I always lose my temper like that."

Peep slowly lifted his head to gaze incredulously at Curt.

"You too?" he said. Slowly, a tear formed and rolled down his nose. "Oh, my poor young friend!"

"Oh, stop it!" said Ellen, exasperated. "Peep, you can't just sit there! We need you!"

Peep jerked his head up to stare at her.

"That's right," said Jim. "The lifeboat opened a hatch and let out a lot of stuff into the cabin, but half of it we can't understand."

"Of course!" Peep struck his head one of his self-punishing sledge-hammer blows with his fist. "My duty! I'm forgetting my duty! Of course, none of you have had ordinary training in things like this, have you?"

"No, we haven't," growled Curt.

Peep jumped to his feet.

"How like a philosopher!" he said chidingly to himself, trotting toward the open hatch of the lifeboat as the other three trotted after him. "Concerned only with his own failings while others are in need." And he disappeared through the hatch. "I'll bring it out!" he called from inside the lifeboat. Jim, Ellen and Curt halted outside.

A moment later, Peep reappeared with his arms full of what appeared to be different-sized black boxes ranging from matchbox dimensions up to one cube about six inches on a side. Peep put these down in a pile at their feet and picked up the smallest box. He passed it to Jim, who was next to him.

"Here," he said. "Put this to your right temple, young friend, make your mind receptive, and relax. In about ten of your seconds, you will get a complete briefing on this world, its peoples, and their customs."

Jim did as he was directed. He stood there while Ellen and Curt watched him, but nothing seemed to happen.

"I don't get anything," he said, handing the box back to Peep.

Peep stared at him, then at the box.

"You don't?" inquired the Atakit. "Strange . . ." He took the box from Jim, pressed it to his own furry skull, and his eyes lit up. After about ten seconds he took it away. "But it's working excellently now, young friend," he said, passing it back to Jim. "Try it again."

Jim did. He stood there, holding the box to his skull and feeling foolish.

"Nothing," he said, handing it over to Curt. Curt tried. He had no luck. Neither did Ellen, when she took the box in her turn.

"Dear me!" said Peep, unhappily. "I wonder if your lack of elementary training deprives you in this respect too, young friends?"

"It certainly looks like it," said Curt. "How can we find our way to the rescue beacon, whatever it is, when we don't know anything about this place—what it's called—"

"Quebahr. I have it!" cried Peep, lighting up. "You need not worry. *I* now know everything about this world. If you wish any information you have only to ask me.''

"Where's the beacon, then?" demanded Curt.

"On the Noif Temple-Island of Annohne," replied Peep, promptly. "You see?" He beamed at them.

"How do we get to it? And how far is it?" asked Jim.

"It is three islands distant," said Peep. "It should take us, I am informed, about nine days by native forms of transportation, to get there. As for those forms, they include walking, riding native animals, and much travel in boats. Naturally, we must be disguised.''

"Disguised?" said Ellen. "Disguised as what?"

Peep turned to beam at her.

"Fortunately, young friend," he said to her, "there is a race native to this world who strongly resemble you humans. They are known as Mauregs. The mechanisms aboard the lifeboat will take care of minor differences. Will you follow me, please?"

He trotted off and into the lifeboat. Somewhat hesitantly, the three others followed him. They found him at the back wall of the compartment behind the second pair of seats.

"Young friends," he said. "Observe."

Bending down, he touched the wall, and at his feet something slid out resembling the drawer of a large filing cabinet, or—the memory came unhappily to Jim's mind of a crime or story he had seen on late television—one of the drawers in a police morgue where corpses are kept cold and preserved.

"Simply lie down in this, one at a time, young friends," Peep said to them.

"I'll flip you to see who goes first," said Curt to Jim. Looking at the tall young man, it occurred to Jim that perhaps Curt had seen the same television bit he had. Curt was slightly pale.

"No," grunted Jim. "What's the use?" He started to get in.

"No. Let me go first, then!" Curt shoved Jim aside. His face was definitely pale, but determined. "I'd like to." He managed to fit his long length into the drawer and looked up at Peep. "I'm ready."

Peep beamed and slid the drawer shut.

"Don't you have to set some controls?" demanded Ellen, nervously.

"No, no," said Peep, cheerfully. "The mechanism will scan our young friend and determine what's to be done—then do it. It's completely automatic." He reached down and slid the drawer open. Curt climbed out. An altered-looking Curt.

Jim and Ellen stared at him.

"Is . . . is that make-up?" Ellen asked. Hesitantly, she reached up to touch one of the two bumps that had appeared on his forehead.

"Make-up?" Curt reached up and touched his own forehead. "What make-up? No . . . that's just my skin, there." He stared around them. "What'd it do to me? How do I look?"

"Different," said Jim.

Curt did indeed look different. As Peep had said, the differences that had made Curt into an apparent Maureg were minor. But they were also startling.

His hair had changed color to a tawny gold. Also, it had disappeared to high up on the sides of his head, so that the result was a sort of wide scalp lock that ran from his forehead back over his skull and down to the nape of his neck. The skin of his body had acquired a golden tinge, and his eyes, instead of their original brown color, had irises now of a green as bright as that of the foliage on the trees above the lifeboat. On either side of Curt's forehead and below the hairline of his scalp lock were two smooth bulges under the skin—like bruise-swellings about two inches in width, except that they were not discolored the way bruises would normally be, but seemed a normal part of his forehead.

"Those protuberances," Peep informed him, as Curt's fingers explored the swellings, "in the normal Maureg represent sensory areas for the perception of ultrasonic vibrations, which function as a sort of radar under certain circumstances when the Maureg makes a high-pitched humming noise. In your case, of course, the protuberances are entirely false. If you will go forward to the screen and request that it become a mirror it will do so, and you can view yourself, young friend."

Curt went off to do this, and Jim lay down in the drawer and was shoved into the wall. Once inside, a voice warned him to keep his eyes closed. There was a second of what seemed bright light seen through his closed eyelids, and then Peep was opening the drawer, and he climbed out.

"Well?" he said. "Do I look like Curt?" And went off to the mirror surface of the screen to check for himself.

He and Curt were still engaged in self-examination when they were politely invited to remove themselves from the lifeboat. Ellen, it seemed, wanted no one in the lifeboat with her but Peep, when she came out of the drawer. Peep seconded the motion.

"Besides, young friends," he said, "you will need to outfit yourselves in native clothing. The largest box outside will supply you with it."

They went out and the door of the airlock closed behind them. Opening the largest of the boxes they discovered a good deal of filmy clothing; a lot more than they would have suspected it to contain. Sorting this out by the simple rule of size, they finally collected two heaps of raiment tailored to their own statures, and proceeded to change into it.

What they ended up wearing, over a pair of loose shorts by way of underclothes, were pairs of loose pants, tight at the ankle and otherwise baggy, and similarly baggy shirts, also tight at the wrist and loose in the sleeves. The shirts had deep-cut v-necks, and both shirt and slacks were white.

Sandals of what looked like pale leather, secured around the ankle by a thong, completed the costume.

"Comfortable, anyway," commented Jim, when they were both outfitted. "Climate seems pretty tropical around here."

"The air's surprisingly dry for an island surrounded by an ocean this way, though," said Curt, sniffing the air. "Have you noticed? And no insects—"

He broke off. Peep had just come out of the airlock. He trotted to the pile of clothing, selected a handful of items and turned back to the ship. As he did so, he glanced at Curt and Jim, and paused.

"Also the sashes and caps, young friends," he commented, and went back into the lifeboat, closing the airlock behind him.

Jim turned and dug into the small pile of clothing that was left. He found what looked like two berets of different size and color. The one that fitted him was green. He put it on, found a length of green cloth, which he proceeded to wrap around his waist, tucking in the end to secure it, and looking over, saw that Curt had similarly outfitted himself in cap and sash of red.

All that was left were two capes, with hooks and eyes to secure one end around the neck. Since one was green and one red, Jim picked up the green one and hooked it about his neck. Curt took the other.

"Well," said Jim, "I guess that does it. You look like a costume-party pirate, and I suppose I do, too."

"These capes are kind of warm," said Curt, "even though they're thin. Do you think . . ."

He paused, turning to face the airlock. Jim turned

also. The airlock door was open and Peep was coming out, followed by a strangely dainty-looking figure. Jim blinked and then recognized it as Ellen, made over to look like a Maureg. She stepped out of the airlock, carefully watching where she put her sandals on the ground.

"You look good!" said Curt, enthusiastically.

Ellen's gaze flashed up from the moss at her feet to Curt's face, and she smiled at him so happily that Jim immediately felt like slugging himself on the forehead, Peep-style. Evidently what Curt had said was just what she had wanted to hear—particularly since she did look good.

She was dressed and made up with the same yellow tinge to the skin and green eyes and forehead bumps that Curt and Jim had. The only difference was that she lacked the scalp lock. She still had all her hair, but it was now curled or waved tight about her head like a golden helmet. It suited her. As far as clothes went, her costume was the same as Jim's and Curt's, except that the neck of the shirt was high and rounded, instead of v-cut, and the trousers were a good deal wider in the legs, so that at first glance they almost looked like a skirt. There was an Earthside name for something like that—a skirt that wasn't; but Jim couldn't think of it at the moment.

He turned his attention to Peep, who was opening other boxes and fitting things together—producing surprisingly large-looking objects out of tiny containers and fitting these together to make still larger objects.

Already lying on the light green, mosslike vegetation covering the ground like a close carpet were what looked like a couple of short, recurved bows, three narrow swords, and three curved daggers. As Jim watched, Peep produced four small knives and a third bow, which he assembled out of four separate pieces that had each unfolded three times to triple their length.

"Help yourselves, young friends," he said.

Jim took a bow, a sword, a dagger, and a knife. He strung the bow and slung it over his shoulder with the bowstring slack. The edged weapons he stuck through his sash. Peep took only the fourth knife, which he strapped to his right forearm.

The dagger had seemed strangely heavy. Jim took it back out of his sash and examined it. The knob on the end of the long, thick handle attracted his attention. He turned it, found it unscrewed, and removed it. The handle was hollow and filled with what seemed to be coppery coins.

"The local style of purse," explained Peep. "All of you, young friends, will find that you are moneyed in this fashion."

"But Peep!" said Ellen. "How about you?" She pointed. "That little knife can't hold anything in the way of coins."

Peep's face changed. It became sad and noble in expression.

"My role on this world," he said, "is not one that permits me to handle money."

"You're a hermit, or something?" asked Curt, interested.

Peep's sad, noble expression gave way to one of slight embarrassment.

"No, indeed," he said, almost guiltily. "Nothing so worthy, young friends. In fact, my role here is— you will notice that I have been altered to appear more hirsute—almost shaggy."

They had not noticed, but he had. Also, his pelt had become a lighter shade of brown, his ears appeared longer, and they were now pointed.

"You three happen to resemble the Maureg people of this planet in appearance," said Peep. "There are, in fact, three intelligent races on this world of Quebahr, instead of only one, as on your Earth. Besides the Mauregs, there are the Walats. Also, there are the Noifs, who most resemble Iguanodon, one of the upright, stalking reptiles of the Mesozoic era in your earth's geological history, sixty to a hundred and eighty million years ago."

"You mean this planet is younger than Earth? I mean," said Jim, "it's still in the dinosaur age?"

"No, indeed. No," said Peep, quickly. "It would be impossible to compare the two worlds in that way. For one thing, an age of reptiles could not have developed here as it did on Earth, since this world has no real continents, only islands in a planet-wide sea. No, the Noifs undoubtedly had a lizardlike ancestor, but you see that they are contemporary here with the humanlike Mauregs. In fact, the Noifs themselves are not cold-blooded, although they had cold-blooded ancestors down to more recent times than did the Mauregs and Walats, but have an internal temperature-regulating mechanism, and a four, rather than a two-chambered pumping organ, or heart. No, they simply resemble Iguanodon, except that they have no spikelike thumb, are much smaller—in fact, slightly smaller than yourselves as a race—and are the equal of you and the Mauregs in intelligence.''

"What's the third race like?" asked Jim. "What did you call them—Walats?"

"The third race," said Peep, lifting his hand, almost like a lecturer, "young friends, are indeed called the Walats. They most resemble your earthly marsupials, being pouched. In fact, they bear their strongest relationship in appearance to the kangaroos of Australia and New Zealand. They are the largest of the three intelligent races on this world."

"How large?" asked Curt.

"The males of the race," answered Peep, "are about as tall as yourself, but they will weigh up to double the amount you do."

"But how about you, Peep?" put in Ellen. "That's what I really want to know. What are you supposed to be?"

Peep looked meekly down at the moss at his feet, before raising his head to answer her.

"I," he said, "—and it is most appropriate, considering my outrageous explosions of temper, my lack of self-control and faulty adherence to the shining principle of nonviolence—most resemble an animal which is one of the semi-intelligent species of which this world has several, in keeping with its multiplicity of intelligent races. This animal is called a bundii and it is famous," said Peep, lowering his gaze to the moss once more, "for its lack of ferocity. Although my size, in its wild state, it is often the prey of other wild animals much smaller than itself."

Peep looked up and around at the faces of the three humans.

"In fact," he continued, earnestly, "a common phrase on Quebahr—particularly among the Walats, who make rather a cult of courage—is, 'cowardly as a bundii.' And I think," concluded Peep, with humility, "it will be very enlightening for me to adopt such a character, young friends."

He waited as if for some answer. None of the three, however, seemed to be able to think of any.

"I will supposedly be your pet, you see," said Peep, driving the fact home. "Perhaps you should make a special effort to call me 'Hey, you!' and give me orders when we practice our roles the rest of today."

"Practice?" asked Jim. "Aren't we going to get going right away?"

"I think," answered Peep, "we should practice our knowledge of the language and use of the weapons, today, then get an early start tomorrow down the side of the mountain to the Port City of Chyk, where we can arrange for a boat to the next island of Hekko.''

"Language!" said Jim, scowling. "We don't know the language, Peep. Maybe you do—"

"Mena'hkim ras suul?" inquired Peep, interrupting him.

"Ha'n ay!" retorted Jim vigorously, making a circle with his upward-pointing right thumb, and then jerking the thumb upward. He started and stared at this thumb in surprise.

Peep had just said in Quebahrian—and Jim had understood him—the equivalent of "you're kidding me!" And Jim had answered, automatically in the same language, "I am not!" The gesture with his thumb had been a sort of hand-signal exclamation point. Now that he was aware of his knowledge of Quebahrian, Jim was as suddenly aware of his knowledge that the language was full of such gestures. It was as active as Italian in that way.

"But when did we learn it?" cried Ellen. For Jim, she, and Curt had also understood what he and Peep had said.

"At the same time you were altered to look like Mauregs," answered Peep. "Language and habits is a different area of learning from the intellectual memorization produced by that little device we tried first. Along with Maureg appearance, you took on the conditioned reflexes of Quebahrian language and custom; luckily, all three races because of their long intermingling speak the same tongue. Observe, young friends"—Peep pointed to their sashes and their bows, swords, and daggers—"how you have arranged your clothing and armament correctly without stopping to think about how you should do it."

It was true, thought Jim, looking at Curt and Ellen. They both wore their clothes and their weapons as if they had been used to them all their lives.

"But," went on Peep, "in spite of your new conditioned reflexes, there is bound to be a certain self-consciousness in using these attributes at first. Which is why I suggest we spend the rest of this day talking and behaving as Quebahrians."

He beamed at them.

"I, too," he said, "must practice the part of a timid bundii, unable to speak more than a few words and not gifted with intelligence. Shall we begin our practice by assuming that we are going into an inn and demanding lodging for the night. Young friend, Jim, suppose you do the talking this first time we act it out, and the tree over there can be the innkeeper . . ."

They began their practicing. It went very well, except that a little over an hour later there was a small noise and a small puff of smoke, as the lifeboat blew up.

It left no trace of its presence. They were now really stranded on Quebahr.

6

They play-acted until dark, made a meal off some provisions among the supplies, and rolled up for the night in their cloaks—which, as Curt had noticed, were surprisingly warm—on the soft moss. The sun woke them early and they headed down the side of the volcano.

As they went, they moved out from under the tall, pinelike trees with all their branches at the top, into an area of shorter trees somewhat like palms. These grew in clumps with little open areas between them, floored not with moss but with some grasslike vegetation. Here they also ran into their first insects, which buzzed about them, but did not bite.

"I'll bet no insects here will bite us," said Ellen.

"We're alien to this world, and that probably means we can't eat them, and the native life can't eat us."

"Who says so?" demanded Curt, crankily, batting at the insects. "Maybe they don't bite, but they get in my ear and buzz. What makes you so sure?"

"It's one of the basic premises of xenobiology," said Ellen, agreeably. Jim frowned at her, puzzled. Not that he had ever been able to understand other people, but he understood girls least of all. On the one hand, Ellen wasn't bothered by other people's growling when he himself would have felt like punching the growler in the nose. On the other hand, some innocent statement, such as he had made about sociology aboard the spaceship, set her off like a rocket.

"Xeno?" Curt was saying.

"Stranger-or-alien biology," Ellen answered. "If it would poison you to eat the alien, then it must poison the alien to eat you . . . and so on. Isn't that right, Peep?"

"Indeed," Peep replied. "The theory is excellent. However, in practice, in this particular case, both you and I can eat the native fruits, vegetables, and meats, though not the fish. There are no freshwater fish on this world and the ocean fish have too high a concentration of potassium oxide in their flesh, for what cause I was not informed."

"Look," said Curt, "there's a trail of some kind slanting off down the slope. Think we ought to follow that?"

"I think," said Peep, judiciously, "that it is probably the most direct route to a full-sized road such as we will want to follow down to the port city of Chyk.''

They took the trail, which plunged them almost immediately into a forest of the palmlike trees. The insects were left behind, but as they wound down the now grassless earth of the hillside under the shade of the palm-needle trees, they spotted a pair of what looked like large bats flying among the branches, and disturbed a piglike creature, which scuttled across the trail in front of them. It was porcine even to boarlike tusks, but had a marsupial-like pouch underneath it from which peered out the tiny tusked heads of two young.

"Well," said Curt, as the trail broadened, approaching a sharp turn around a thick clump of trees, "we seem to be getting closer to civilization."

He had barely finished saying this before they rounded the turn and found themselves walking down the main street, about fifty yards long, of a native village. Jim, in the lead, saw an adult male Maureg rise suddenly from before one of the thatch-roofed sapling-sided huts that lined the street, and vanish inside it. He took with him something that Jim only glimpsed—it was black, about three feet long and looked oddly like a cross with a crooked long member and the two ends of the crosspiece not in line with each other.

Jim had a sudden feeling of uneasiness. Up until now he had been lulled to the point of nearly forgetting that they were strangers on an unknown and possibly hostile world. Now he was suddenly and vividly reminded of it. He found himself wishing that they had gone around the village.

However, there was no chance of that now. The only thing to do was keep on down the street, past the stream that crossed the road and pooled up into what was obviously the village fountain, and so out of the village and on their way.

As they proceeded to do just that, however, the appearance of the village changed. None of the villagers seemed to pay Jim and his party any particular attention, and none of them moved suddenly after the disappearance of the first individual carrying the odd, crosslike object. But gradually all the women and children drifted into the huts, and the men drifted out. As Jim led the others toward the fountain and the open forest at the end of the village, he heard Peep murmuring quietly at his elbow.

"Young friend," said Peep. "I think it would be wise to stop and at least pretend to drink from their fountain. This is a gesture symbolic of trust and friendliness among the Mauregs. It gives them a chance to question the strangers among them."

"If you say so," muttered Jim. He turned his head a little to the right. "Ellen, is your bowstring cased?"

"Yes," murmured the voice of Ellen. "But I don't think I ought to string the bow now, do you?"

"No, I guess not," said Jim, grimly. It had developed during their play-acting and practice yesterday that they had, for practical purposes, only one weapon among them. Ellen, who looked small enough to have trouble opening an Earth-style can of sardines, turned out to be an expert archer and a dead shot with her bow. It had rubbed Curt's ego the wrong way until he discovered that what little he knew of fencing was decidedly more than the knowledge in that department that Jim possessed—which was nothing.

"Maybe we ought to stop and draw our swords," said his voice in Jim's ear, now.

Jim's temper, already set on hair trigger by the tense situation, flared. Of all the Archaist nonsense—to start waving around weapons none of them knew how to use in the face of superior numbers of natives who probably knew how to use them only too well! That was Curt all right.

Turning around to snap at the tall young man under his breath, Jim saw that the other's face was fixed and determined, but pale and with a glisten of sweat on the forehead. It struck Jim that Curt was not perhaps aching for the chance to wave a sword around after all; that the other might be one of those who throw themselves into things for fear of being betrayed by their own forebodings. Jim decided not to snap.

"No swords," he answered. "We're at the fountain anyway. Just stop."

They halted and turned toward the pool of the fountain, which was a circular stone cup with a white clay lining, set in the side of a four-foot-high artificial dam over which the stream plunged.

"It's quite safe to actually drink, young friends," Peep murmured, and suited his words by taking up a double handful of the cold water and drinking it. The rest followed his example. As Jim was lifting his head from his emptied and dripping palms, a voice spoke in his left ear, softly.

"O Friend . . ."

He turned around. He, Peep, and the others were surrounded by perhaps a dozen and a half fully armed Maureg men. There were no women or children in sight at all. The group showed no sign of anger or hostility, but Jim's conditioned Quebahrian reflexes stiffened him. Whether they were expressing it or not, the Mauregs of this village were not happy with the presence of strangers.

"Good day, Friends," answered Jim in Quebahrian. They would have to pick on me, the slowest talker and thinker of the group, he thought. Why is it always me at times like this? "This is fine water you've got here."

"Drink, and be welcome," said the Quebahrian facing Jim. He was slim, lighter than Jim and no taller—in fact the Mauregs in general were lighter-framed than the humans—nor was there any way of judging his age. His smooth, yellowish face under its scalp lock gave no clue. But there was an air of authority implying maturity about him. "You're strangers here on the volcano side."

"That's right," answered Jim. The other's words had been no question, but a calm statement of fact. "We're on our way down to the sea—to the port city."

"To Chyk? You aren't from Chyk. You're not from this island."

How in blazes would he know that? wondered Jim.

"From Hekko," he said shortly, dredging up the name of the next island to which Peep had said they were headed. "Just visiting here."

"But you are up on the volcano side?"

He wants to know what we're doing here, thought Jim, staring the other grimly in the eye. And I haven't got a reason ready for him. But at this moment Peep took a hand.

"I lost," he announced, in an outrageous voice that could only be described, impossible as it sounded, as a bass squeak.

"Yes," said Jim gratefully, keeping his eyes locked on the eyes of his Maureg questioner. "Our bundii wandered off from Chyk, and we've been hunting him for several days now. We just found him last night. But it was too late to try to get back, so we slept out and started back down this morning. We found your road here, a little way back up the slope."

"Indeed," said the Maureg, glancing for a second at Peep, "you have a bundii. And bundiis do become fearful when left alone and run from dangers that are not there until they get lost."

"O Friend," said Jim, taking the bull by the horns and scowling at his questioner, "you don't doubt what I say, do you?"

"O Friend," replied the other, "why should I doubt you? But you said that you had found your bundii, and indeed we can see that you've found him, and no doubt now you will be anxious to return to Chyk.''

''Indeed,'' said Jim. ''And from Chyk we'll be leaving for Hekko as soon as we can find a boat going there. The sun is almost overhead at noon, and probably it's best if we get going.''

''O Friend,'' said the Maureg, ''that is a wise decision. May the triple gods guard you as you go and find you a boat quickly so that you may leave Chyk. I have a premonition that such will be the case and that the voyage will be lucky for being swift.''

''Then farewell, O Friend,'' said Jim, beginning to back away toward the woods beyond the bridge at his back that marked the lower limits of the village. He was happy to note that Ellen, Curt, and Peep were moving with him. ''Thank you for your water.''

''It was our honor and pleasure to have you drink it,'' said the Maureg. He and his friends were drifting along as the humans and Peep backed away. They followed, the Maureg exchanging polite phrases with Jim until the sandal-heels of Curt, who was farthest behind Jim, rang hollow on the planks of the little bridge.

Then the Mauregs halted and watched as their visitors backed across the bridge, bowed a final good-bye and, reaching at last the edge of the lower woods, turned and went.

''Whew!'' said Curt, when they were at last out of earshot of the village. ''What'd we do wrong?''

"I don't know, young friend," said Peep, sounding badly puzzled. "Their attitude did not agree at all with what I understood from the briefing mechanism that gave me knowledge of this world. I was given to understand that while in past centuries there had been fighting between the different intelligent species—Maureg, Walat, and Noif—for control of various islands, nowadays they all lived amicably together. And there has never been warfare or strife between those of the same species. The briefing seems out of date."

"They were hiding something back in that village. Something they thought we'd find out about," said Ellen energetically. "I know it."

"What do you think, Jim?" asked Curt.

"Don't know," muttered Jim. "Anyway, we got out of it all right and with luck we'll be off this island tonight."

"Oh, I hardly think quite that fast, young friends," said Peep. "Even if we reach Chyk by midafternoon and find a ship to Hekko that will take us, it will have to wait for the morning tide. I understand that the Mauregs, who do most of the shipping between islands, are mainly day-sailors. They heave to and drift at night."

"That so?" said Jim, absently. In fact, his mind was elsewhere. He was thinking that from the moment he had stepped aboard the spaceship things had been happening most strangely. First, there had been the odd business of Ellen being allowed to watch the spaceship take-off while he and Curt were locked in their staterooms. Then the spaceship had broken down when that was supposed to be next to impossible. Now the natives of this planet were acting in a way that, according to Alien information, they were not supposed to be acting.

It could hardly, thought Jim, be a sort of Alien plot against the three humans, because Peep was as much a victim of it if that was so, as he, Ellen, and Curt were victims. How the Federation was composed of the Aliens had never been said. But it must contain many different races and types of intelligent beings.

"Tell me, Peep," said Jim, suddenly, "do the different races, or peoples as you call them, get along well together in the Federation? Or do they sometimes have opposite points of view about things?"

Peep hesitated.

"Young friend," he said, "I was told before leaving Earth that no one had better attempt to explain Federation conditions to you until you had completed your basic education. So perhaps I should not answer that. But surely logic should show you that where you have even two individual attitudes, they must be in opposition, if not conflict, on *some* points."

Jim nodded. Peep's answer went a long way to feed the suspicion that had recently begun to sprout in the back of his mind.

The slope they descended was leveling out now, and the trail was widening into a road wide enough to accommodate small carts—if they existed on the islands of Quebahr. Shortly, they emerged altogether from the trees and found themselves traversing the gentle swell and dip of farm lands sloping from the foot of the volcanic cone toward the sea.

The road widened rapidly as the farm lands on either side flattened. Shortly the road, although it remained unpaved, acquired a drainage ditch on either side, perceptible shoulders, and other evidence of construction and upkeep. They passed several roadside communities of Mauregs, but these paid little or no attention to them. By midafternoon they came over a small rise and saw a hazy blue line in the distance that was the sea.

From this point they could see ahead down a gentle hollow to a thickening of buildings. Most of the buildings so far had been huts with pole frames, thatched roofs, and walls made of slim sticks tied side by side into panels, which were also tied together, to make what were really large, airy screens, rather than walls in the Earthly sense. Now in the distance they saw rising from among clusters of huts larger buildings made of some solid material. In the far distance, against the sea, was the black outline of the buildings of a community of size and importance.

They went on, with Curt, who had acquired a blister on his right heel, limping a little; and a little more than an hour later, they were moving into the shadow of the community they had seen—two- and three-story structures of mud-brick or even timber with blank fronts and high walls all around them.

"I'll bet they've got courtyards, fountains, and gardens inside those walls," said Ellen.

Jim looked sideways and down at her in surprise.

"How do you know?" he asked.

"Oh, just some of my sociological guesswork," she answered, airily. "This resembles a type of construction common in the Latin countries of the Western Hemisphere—and in the lands around the Mediterranean."

"Roman," said Curt, hastily. "Actually, it started with the Romans—say, I'll bet if we had a legion of trained Roman infantry, we could conquer this world with no trouble at all!"

"I wouldn't count on it, young friend—" Peep began, when Ellen broke in.

"Just a minute before you get started, Peep, please," she said. "Was I right about the courtyards and gardens?"

"As a matter of fact, young friend," said Peep, beaming at her with almost fatherly pride, "you were."

"I just wanted to find out," said Ellen, throwing a triumphant glance at Jim.

What did I do? I just asked, thought Jim, puzzled.

"Go on with what you were going to say," added Ellen to Peep.

"I was going to say," said Peep, "that in spite of our young friend's optimism," he looked benevolently up at Curt, towering beside him as they walked, "it would probably be a mistake to believe that your

Roman legionnaires, excellent soldiers that they were, would have little difficulty in subduing all of Quebahr. I would like to point out that we have as yet been only in the environs—out in the sticks, as it were—of this one island. Further, we have so far met only the Mauregs, who on this island form the major part of the population. And the Mauregs are by nature artisans and artists, fishers and farmers."

"What are the other two like?" asked Jim.

"The Walats are boisterous and combative," said Peep. "Originally they were nomads, with a typical nomadic culture of movement, warfare, and pillage. Nowadays they most often find occupation as police or mercenary soldiers for the Noifs. The Noifs, though physically the smallest of the three intelligent races here, are strongly scientific-minded. In fact, in an ingrown fashion, they are quite advanced scientifically. Your legionnaires, young friend," wound up Peep, glancing at Curt, "might find little trouble with the Mauregs, but they would not find the going easy with the Walats, or even the Noifs."

"You say so, but I'll believe it when I see it," retorted Curt argumentatively. "Do you know that counterparts of the Roman short sword and locked shields were able to destroy in Spain the massed pikes of Swiss-type infantry that had sounded the downfall of the medieval armored horse and rider? Why, they—"

He broke off. The street they had been following between buildings several stories high had just narrowed and been roofed over to make a high gateway. The gates were ajar, but on either side of the gateway stood individuals of a kind they had not yet encountered, but which their new Quebahrian reflexes instantly recognized, even if Peep's description had not prepared them to do so. The individuals were guards and the guards were Walats.

As Peep had said, they looked something like Earthly kangaroos. But the resemblance was an overall, superficial resemblance. Actually, they were much more erect than kangaroos, with larger skulls, forearms more developed and enlarged, and legs less developed in kangaroo fashion for leaping. Perhaps the greatest resemblance lay in the fact they had tails; which, kangaroo fashion, balanced the forward angle of their upper bodies.

But they were *big*. Tall, heavy, and powerful. They wore kilts, boots, and upper shirts like the Mauregs, but over this was a leather harness from which depended a small arsenal of weapons, including one sword double the weight and length of the one Jim was carrying. The biceps of their arms bulged out their sleeves like the biceps of weight lifters. They lounged about the gateway, gazing with a sort of good-natured contempt at the Mauregs passing through, among whom walked the three disguised humans, and Peep.

It was disconcerting, Jim found, to be looked at with contempt by a pair of dark and unexpectedly intelligent eyes in a huge, lolling creature that looked like one of Earth's lower animals, transported to a different world. What if they stop us and question us? he thought suddenly. We should have figured out what to say in advance.

But the Walats showed no desire to question anyone passing through the gate. And, in fact, the three humans and Peep were almost through and Jim was beginning to breathe easier, when out of the corner of his eye he caught the flash of something long and metallic.

Peep squealed in his bundii-type basso-squeak, and scuttled around to the other side of Jim. Turning, Jim saw one of the Walats grinning along the length of his long mouth and sliding his outsized sword back into its sheath.

Jim stopped.

"Now, wait a minute," he said, scowling at the Walat. The other's grin vanished and, turning to face Jim, he checked his sword while it was still only halfway back in its sheath. But Jim felt his sleeve tugged, and looked down to see Peep.

"Please, master!" squeaked Peep. "No fight!" He winked hard at Jim.

Jim woke suddenly to the fact that his sense of outrage was threatening to endanger them all. His ears burning, he turned and went off with Peep and the others, hearing behind him the deep-voiced coughing laughter of the Walat he had almost unthinkingly challenged.

"You see, young friend," said Peep, urgently,

once they were safely around a corner and free from observers who might find it odd to hear a bundii speaking intelligently, "it is merely typical of the Walat sense of humor, that one should wish to frighten a timid animal such as I am supposed to be. That guard meant no harm. By law, he is forbidden to steal or damage anyone's property, and I am supposed to be your property. Only a real bundii would not know this, and so I had to act terrified when he drew his sword and menaced me."

"You're right. You're absolutely right," said Jim, contritely. "I don't know what I was thinking I could do. On top of everything else I don't know one end of a sword from the other and he's probably an expert with that buffalo-sticker of his—"

Curt stopped suddenly in the middle of the street, so that Jim bumped into him from behind. They all stopped and stared at him.

"Peep!" said Curt. "Would it be against the Federation rules if I got myself a wooden staff and carried it?"

"I can't conceive why it should be," said Peep, obviously puzzled. "But why?"

"Let me ask you another question. Do they know anything on this world about quarterstaves?"

"Quarterstaves? No," answered Peep. "What is a quarterstave, young friend?"

"Quarterstaff!" corrected Curt, excitedly. "Just the most powerful and dangerous hand weapon ever devised, that's all it is!"

"Do you know how to use one?" asked Jim, skeptically.

"Well, no," said Curt, with determination. "But once I read a book that had something on it. We can get a couple of staves and practice between ourselves. There's no point trying to learn how to use a sword in a few days when people on this world will have been using them all their lives. Peep—where can we get some lengths of seasoned wood, rods about an inch to two inches thick and about six or eight feet long—tipped with iron, if possible."

"A local smith will make metal caps for such rods," said Peep. "But where to get the rods themselves puzzles me. Perhaps . . . but in any case our first job is to arrange for passage on some ship to Hekko. And to do that we must first see the harbor master. According to my briefing, the route to his office should be just the way we're headed at the moment. So, let us be on our way."

He trotted off, and the others followed him. He led them down twisting streets between high buildings, some of which had booths in front where Mauregs displayed pottery or leather goods for sale. Shortly, they came to the waterfront, with its long quays sticking out over the dark water of the harbor and a horde of strangely flat-looking ships with stubby sails at anchor. Peep led them along the waterfront to a large building constructed of dark stone blocks and into what was obviously some sort of office. There was a high bench running around the walls of the room, littered with papers. Standing at this bench was a Maureg, and at the sight of them he stopped fussing with some of the papers and came over.

"O Friends," he said, and his eyes moved sharply from one to the other of them, not omitting even Peep, "can I be of service?"

"Well," said Jim, when no one else seemed about to speak up, "we want to get to Hekko."

"Yes," said the Maureg, slightly hissing the word. It was almost as if he said *"Ah-hah!"* like a villain in an old-fashioned melodrama. "You will need to receive the permission of the harbor master. The harbor master may or may not charge you a fee. For myself, I charge no fees. I am a poor man, but I would never think of asking anyone who came in here for a fee. Of course, there are those who thrust fees upon me . . ."

Jim caught on—it did not take the most perceptive person of Quebahr to do so. He drew his curved dagger, unscrewed the knob and extracted two coins which he gave to the clerk, or whatever he was.

"Noble friend! I thank you. The harbor master will see you now. Go right in through that farther door, there. Just at the moment, I, myself, am called away."

The speaker turned and glided past them out the door of the office to the steps and the street. Puzzled, replacing the knob on his dagger in his belt, Jim led the others into the farther room. He found it a smaller place full of what looked like large cabinets or filing cases. There was no one to be seen.

"Hello!" called Jim, "is the harbor master here?"

"I am the harbor master," answered an invisible speaker, who a second later came around a nearby filing cabinet to face them, with dark, clever, and coldly penetrating eyes. They stared back.

They were face to face with their first Noif.

7

The Noif was less than five and a half feet tall, only a little taller than Ellen. He was dark and smoothly skinned, and did indeed resemble a miniature of the Iguanodon Jim had once seen in a geology textbook. The differences were not so much that he was less lizardlike, but that he was more upright of body, lacked a tail, and his head and face were much more humanoid, except for the wide and lipless mouth. He wore only a sort of leather kilt with a small knife holstered in it.

Other than the small knife—it was an eating utensil, actually, Peep had informed them the day before—that was like the one every other inhabitant of Quebahr carried, the Noif harbor master was not armed in any way, except for a strange device slung over one dark shoulder by a leather sling. This was black, had a tube at one end, a stock at the other, and above and below the trigger housing in the near middle, were two projections—one up, one down, off-center from each other—that looked like cartridge holders.

In fact the whole assembly bore a strange resemblance to the British Sten submachine guns of World War II or the American M3, only with another long cartridge clip above the barrel as well as the one below. Jim tried to get a good look at it without obviously staring, but as it hung down behind the Noif's back it was difficult to catch more than occasional glimpses. Jim was ready to swear, however, that it was an object like this that the Maureg had gotten swiftly out of sight when they had stumbled across the village on the volcano's side earlier in the day. The connection made him suddenly uneasy.

"O Friends," said the Noif, quietly, "what service can the harbor master render you?"

Jim pulled himself together.

"We're looking for a ship on which we can hire passage to Hekko," he said.

"Interesting," said the harbor master. His dark eyes examined each of them and came back to Jim. There was a remote, coolly speculative look in those eyes that examined them as if they were things to be taken apart and studied. Jim had seen something like it somewhere before—he could not remember where—and the very familiarity put him more at ease than he otherwise would have been.

"This is convenient for you," said the harbor master. "A ship owner has just left my office here, who is sailing for Hekko on tomorrow's early tide. He is a Maureg named Llalal, and his ship is at one of the quays."

The harbor master stopped speaking and went back to examining them with his remote, speculative glance. He seemed content to stand there forever, so Jim spoke up.

"What's the fee?" he asked. And although the natural flourishes of the Quebahrian language did something to mask the bluntness of his question, that bluntness was still apparent.

"I have decided," said the harbor master, "there will be no fee, since you and he came so opportunely together to my office. His ship is called *Llalal's Own*. It is at the end of Quay Four. You should find him on it, or at an inn not too far away."

"Thank you," said Jim, making a belated effort to smooth over his bluntness.

"You need not thank me," said the harbor master. "I have done nothing which could not have been performed for a fee. Since I did not require a fee, I do not require to be thanked. May your voyage be fortunate and *your* triple gods smile upon you, O Maureg Friends."

Jim opened his mouth, but his conditioned Quebahrian reflexes for once seemed at a loss to come up with a properly flowery answer. Rather than say the wrong thing, he said nothing. He bowed and backed

away, leading the other three members of his party
out. The Noif stood gazing steadily at them as they
went.

The Maureg shipowner, Llalal, was not on his
ship, *Llalal's Own,* when they finally found it. The
third waterfront inn they tried admitted that he was
on their premises. The innkeeper showed them into
the back room, half sleeping chamber, half dining
place which Llalal was renting.

He got up from the carpet on which he was squatted, eating from an assortment of dishes, as they
entered. It was the Maureg they had encountered in
the outer office of the harbor master. He began talking rapidly the moment he saw them.

"O Friends," he said, "what could I do? I am a
poor man and you might easily have been sent by the
harbor master to some other ship owner. Of course,
now that you've come to me, the small fee you
offered me will be deducted from the cost of your
passage to Hekko—"

"Just tell me one thing," said Jim, interrupting
him, "why didn't you tell us you were headed for
Hekko when we saw you there?"

"O Friend, what if the harbor master wished to
send you with some other ship? Wouldn't he think I
was intruding on his right to pick the shipowner who
would take you? Come, Friends, I have been uncivil.
I will cut my regular price to—"

"Nothing," Jim finished for him. Llalal stared at
him, open-mouthed.

"You heard me," said Jim. He was feeling rather sore over the trick the other one had played. "Or shall we go back to the harbor master and tell him how you got a fee out of us by posing as someone connected with his office?"

Jim had expected a storm of protest, more bargaining, and a final settlement which should not be too much more than the regular price. What happened surprised him even more.

Llalal got his mouth closed.

"What can I say?" he asked calmly. "Let it be nothing, then. We sail on the morning tide, which is before sunrise. If you stay at this inn, I will wake you. Or you may spend the night on my ship. Do you know where it is?"

Jim found himself scowling at the Maureg suspiciously. He was about to choose the inn, when he felt his sleeve unobtrusively tugged.

"Ship? Ship?" squeaked Peep, bundii-style.

"Yes, yes, bundii," said Jim. He turned back to Llalal. "We'll stay on your ship, come to think of it. We don't want our bundii wandering off."

"Excellent," said Llalal. "I will take you out myself and pass you by the watchman, and see you settled on board."

He did just that, after eating a few more mouthfuls from the dishes spread on the carpet. The sun had descended with tropical suddenness by the time he brought them aboard, and with the help of the watchman from the quay, had rigged partitions of stick panels such as they had seen in the village huts, to make individual rooms for them on deck under the awning that ran sternwards from the foot of the main mast of the ship. Then, having built them staterooms, so to speak, he wished them a pleasant sleep, and went back ashore. To his inn, Jim presumed. They were left alone aboard a sixty-foot craft rocking gently on the dark waters which were now beginning to be illuminated by the faint rays of small twin moons rising in the sky, opposite to that quarter in which the sun had descended.

They made an emergency meal out of the last of the field provisions supplied them by the lifeboat, and turned into their individual deck-staterooms. Jim would not ordinarily have thought of himself as able to wind up the activities of the day at only an hour or two past sunset. But the day's tramp had been more exercise than he realized. He curled up in his cape and drifted off to sleep to the sound of water slapping softly at the side of *Llalal's Own,* only a few feet from where his head lay upon the carpet provided for him.

Dimly, sometime later while it was still dark, he was aware of the sound of feet and voices, the ship beginning a slow and steady rolling from side to side, and the creak and groan of cordage overhead. But he drifted back off into slumber, and did not rouse again until he woke with the dazzle of sunlight through the grating of sticks on the side of his compartment, bright in his eyes.

He lay still for a moment, getting his bearings while his mind gradually brightened into wakefulness. The sunlight through the thin bars of the sticks in the panel-wall of his enclosure made a moving pattern of bright stripes on the carpet in front of his nose. As often happened to Jim, while he was sleeping his mind had come up with the answer to a question that he had not been able to answer the day before.

He remembered now where he had seen that coolly curious, analytical gaze of the Noif, or something very like it, before. It had been in the eyes of Jason Wells and some of the other physicists on the Project at Research Three, back on Earth.

The Noif had had the look of a scientist—of a research man. What was it Peep had said? Yes, it had been something to the effect that while the Mauregs were artistic and the Walats warlike, the Noifs were scientific-minded. And that raised again the deeper question that had been in Jim's mind from the moment he had begun to meet his fellow-travelers aboard the Alien spaceship.

It had only been four, no, five days ago (it seemed more like five centuries) that he had had the argument with Ward Stuyler in his own garage back on Earth, about odds. He had told Ward that he didn't believe in chance or luck. Well, he still didn't. And chance, in the present instance, was getting shoved beyond the point of believability.

Jim had been ready to believe that he could be one out of millions that just fitted the Alien specifications for a chance to study out among the stars. But now that long-odds happening had had three other such happenings piled on top of it. First was the matter of the strangeness of the two other selected humans and Peep . . .

Jim checked himself for a moment at that point. There might be one exception to that. The more he saw of Ellen, the more ready he was to believe that she might be unusual enough to deserve to be chosen against the odds they had all faced. She was a bright light as far as brain went; she had more common sense than you could shake a stick at; and it was becoming more evident all the time that she was not just someone who talked sociology, biology, and anthropology. She actually knew something about these—well, they were sciences, even if so-called "soft" sciences. Now wait a minute, Jim called his brain to order. Biology's a hard science. Come to think of it, maybe anthropology is, too.

All right, assume Ellen was all right. Stretch a few points, give Curt credit for a pretty good set of brains, and some fairly solid knowledge of history, weapons, and so forth. That suggestion of his about quarterstaves had been sound. Suppose Peep's all right—though it was hard to imagine an Alien being that much of a cultist, with his nonviolence. Assume that there was some good reason for not letting him and Curt see the spaceship's take-off. That still left two completely unbelievable strokes of chance.

Item: the spaceship's cracking up, which according

to Peep was never supposed to happen. And, item: the fact that the briefing device had not contained complete or up-to-date information about the situation here on Quebahr.

That many unbelievable chance happenings were simply too much to swallow. Therefore, they couldn't be strokes of chance. They must have been deliberately caused—and if deliberately caused, they must be part of a plan. A plan to do what? Well, evidently to somehow mess up or wreck the Human-Students-Out-to-the-Stars Plan. And who would want to do something like that? No humans could, certainly, even if they wanted to do so.

That left only the Aliens themselves or, more properly, some group or combination among the Alien Federation's population. Peep evidently suspected no such thing, but then Peep was what people of former times on Earth called an Innocent—someone obviously gentle and harmless, but not to be held wholly responsible for his actions.

Jim had asked Peep if there were differences of opinion among people or races or individuals in the Alien Federation, and Peep had as good as admitted that there were. So that checked out.

Jim, Ellen, Curt, and by accident, Peep, therefore, were pretty certainly squarely behind an eightball setup by some unknown Alien group. They could almost certainly expect to run into some pretty nasty trap somewhere between here and when they left Quebahr—more probably, between here and the beacon they must activate to summon their rescuers. The question was, what to do about it?

Jim stared at the bars of sunlight on the rug, swaying with the rolling of the ship. There was not much use talking to Ellen or Curt about it until he had some kind of definite proof of what he had reasoned out, or until their help was needed to deal with the matter. Right now, Ellen would undoubtedly not believe him, and Curt would simply take it as one more proof of his Archaist suspicions of all Aliens. Curt, in fact, would probably insist that it was a plot of the whole Federation against the three of them and turn the business into a farce.

Peep, as had been noted, was an Innocent. There was no point in taking him into Jim's confidence.

Which leaves just me, thought Jim in mild surprise. Come to think of it, that was the way he might expect it to be. Himself alone against some organization of inconceivably well-equipped and informed Aliens. Well, if that was the way it was to be, then so be it.

Surprisingly, having thought this, Jim found himself feeling not uncheerful about the whole matter. At any rate, he had the trouble pinpointed, and the enemy identified. At least he would not go down without a fight. Suddenly realizing he was hungry, Jim sat up, put on his sandals, and crawled out of his "stateroom," feeling optimistic and wide-awake.

He found Ellen, Curt, and Peep a few minutes later, seated in a little open space toward the stern of the vessel on a larger rug decorated with various fruits, dishes containing what looked like cooked food, and a large earthenware vessel resembling an enormous pitcher with its top sealed over.

"Hi," said Curt cheerfully, breaking off from the conversation to lift his head at the sound of Jim's sandals on the plank deck. "Join us. Breakfast in front of you. See if you can find something that doesn't taste funny to you. Water in the pitcher—it comes from holes under the spout. Look out!"

Jim joined them and set about finding himself a breakfast from the available foods. As Curt had said, they all touched strangely against his human palate. But he found one fruit and a couple of the cooked dishes that were not bad, and he became more practiced in handling the "pitcher" skillfully so that the water did not all go up his nose or down his neck. Meanwhile the other three went back to what was apparently Peep's lecture on the good effects of practicing nonviolence.

Jim paid no attention at first, but as he finished up his breakfast, he found himself listening.

". . . Since that inexcusable lapse aboard the spaceship," Peep was saying to Ellen and Curt, beaming, "I have not been tempted once. Observe, I have not merely not lost control of my emotions, I have not been *tempted* to do so. I feel that I have finally managed to develop a new attitude of gentleness toward all beings. I woke up early this morning and saw a large fish near the ship. I sat watching him and practiced loving and nonviolent thoughts in his direction. Will you believe it? He is still following. It is too much to hope for, of course, but I am half convinced that he senses my gentleness and affection toward him and desires to stay with us for that reason. Why else should he stay with us all this time?''

"Looks something like a shark," said Curt, glancing over the side at a tall black fin that was dogging the vessel.

"You think so?" Peep looked also. "It does," he said anxiously, "somewhat resemble your Earthly shark. Nonetheless . . ."

"Maybe it's just hungry," said Curt. "Waiting for a sailor to fall overboard." He picked up one of the untouched dishes and emptied its contents over the side. The black fin darted forward, there was a flash of huge teeth, and the water bubbled and swirled where the food had gone overboard.

"Yes," said Peep, sadly. "There seems to be something in what you say. Still, the principle of nonviolence remains sound. You see, young friends, nonviolence is anchored in the concept of complete responsibility. If I feel a proper and total sense of responsibility for the welfare of every other living creature, how can I conceive of violence toward it? Obviously I cannot, for all of us, living creatures, are more alike than we think."

"Which reminds me," said Jim, having finished his breakfast, "I don't know about the rest of you, but it's hard to believe that the people on this world can have so many things that are just like those on Earth. Look—clothing, knives, bows, ships, sails. I can see something basic like—well, like physics being the same on worlds that are as much alike as this and Earth, but the rest of it seems too good to be true.''

"But there is a physics of Life, too, young friend," said Peep. "For example, on an Earth type world the quadruped animal with a four-chambered heart and internal temperature control, such as Earthly mammals have, is the most efficient living form. On different types of worlds, of course, life takes different forms. But here, as on Earth, the quadruped naturally evolved, who, on gaining intelligence, needed to use its front paws as hands, and so learned to stand erect and so on, until a roughly manlike creature emerged—or, I might say, Atakitlike, if I wished to be parochial in my attitude.''

"That's right," said Ellen. "Biology relates to environment. And once you have a manlike intelligent animal, he's going to encounter manlike problems. He'll need housing, he'll want decoration, he'll need to store food and drink and so on.''

"And you talk about weapons," broke in Curt, eagerly. "How many weapons do you think are possible on a simple mechanical level? There are three orders of levers, right, depending on where the fulcrum is placed?''

"Right," said Jim, astonished to find the lanky Archaist knowing anything so sensible.

"All right, think of weapons as levers for exerting

force against an object or an enemy. What do we have? First, on the most primitive level, there's a rock or stick, held or thrown to hit somebody. In either case, whether it's held or thrown, it's an example of a third-order lever with the force being exerted between the fulcrum, which is at the shoulder joint of the arm holding the weapon, and the weight of the stick or stone itself. Do you follow me?''

"So far," said Jim, cautiously.

"All right, a stone pointed and sharpened becomes a knife. A stick pointed and sharpened becomes a spear, and thickened and given a heavy head it becomes a war club. From knives inevitably come daggers and swords. From spears come lances and pikes and so forth. From clubs with sharpened metal heads come axes and from axes, halberds and the like.''

"What about a bow and arrow?" asked Jim.

"A bow and arrow is a slighty complex version of a second-order lever," said Curt, "with the fulcrum at the center of the bowstave itself, and the force exerted backward at the tips by the pulled bowstring against the stiffness of the bowstave. If you want an example of a first-order lever among weapons, there was the trebuchet, a long pivoted arm with a weight on its short end and a cup or container for a missile on its long end. You pulled down the long end, put the missile in the cup, and released the lever. The weight at the short end pulled the arm down, and the missile end flew up in the air, throwing the missile forward.''

Curt stopped talking. Jim stared at him. The lanky young man had just gone up several notches in Jim's opinion.

"Well," said Jim, after a moment. "I guess you're right and I'm wrong. In fact, I know you're right and I'm wrong. I stand corrected."

"Oh, well," said Curt, uncomfortably. He got quickly to his feet. "While I think of it, and now that the subject's come up, I think I'll go ask Llalal if he's got some wooden staves in his cargo we can make into quarterstaves. Want to come?"

"Sure do," said Jim. They went back toward the cargo area of the ship, together.

To Jim's surprise, Llalal did have staves. The surprise dwindled when he saw the rag-bag assortment of cargo carried by *Llalal's Own*. The ship itself was built on the order of a Chinese junk or rather, like an oversize sampan. It was essentially a floating raft with a keel and built-up sides. This meant it had no hold. Below the planks on which everyone stood, slept, and moved about there was nothing but several layers of logs pegged and tied together with a form of Quebahrian wire. This was why the timbers of the ship's body made so much noise rubbing against each other every time the ship rolled.

Therefore, the cargo was carried on deck, piled helter-skelter. The practice of such ships evidently was to load up on whatever was salable at each port and sell off as much as possible of what they were already carrying. For such trade, variety was the spice of business. *Llalal's Own* was consequently nothing much more than a sailing junkyard. Llalal, located having lunch with his two crewmen—by Earth standards the ship was villainously undermanned—got up, rooted around, and came up with a couple of twelve-foot poles an inch and a half in diameter, which could be cut down and used.

Jim bargained only perfunctorily over the cost of the poles, figuring he had probably twisted the Maureg's arm unfairly in the matter of their passage money. Then he and Curt padded the ends of the quarterstaves and set about working out their use.

In the remaining three days before they arrived at Hekko Port, they got rather good at it. They discovered that speed was as important as it was in fencing, which prompted Curt to remember that quarterstaves had been used as a training method for early swordplay. They also discovered that there were all sorts of effective ways to disable a man with a quarterstaff besides hitting him over the head with it; in spite of the fact that Robin Hood and his merry men, judging from their conversation about the quarterstaff, had all been headhunters. Finally, they found out that, even with ends padded to the size of footballs, a quarterstaff could batter and bruise you up considerably.

"I think you like having black eyes," observed Ellen, after the first two days of this. She stayed away from their practice sessions, out of what Jim was beginning to suspect was a much stronger dislike of seeing people hurt than she wished to admit. Peep, after one experience, also stayed away. After five minutes of watching, his eyes had started to redden, his whiskers to twitch and his hands to grasp longingly at the air, as if closing around an imaginary quarterstaff.

"Forgive me, young friends," he said humbly, taking his departure, "but I find I am still somewhat unfit when faced with the temptation to do violence."

Llalal and his two Maureg crew watched interestedly. Jim had told them that it was a sport. He did not know whether they had swallowed this or not, but when at last they pulled into Hekko Port and tied up at one of the quays there, Llalal touched him on the arm as the three humans and Peep were preparing to leave the boat.

"Where do you go now?" he asked, his eyes steady on Jim's face. Gradually during the voyage, the shipowner's character had changed subtly from that of a slippery and unethical trader to that of someone more responsible and thoughtful. "I can help by recommending individuals in all lines of activity."

"Haven't made up our minds yet," said Jim, gruffly. In spite of the other's change in character, he was not going to take any chances. He turned to follow Curt, Ellen, and Peep, who were already on the quay.

Llalal caught his arm. Jim turned back.

"Brother," said Llalal, using that intimate and

friendly form of address for the first time, "no individual can see into the heart of a mountain, but neither can one see to the bottom of the sea."

The words rang strangely on Jim's ear. There was something about the way Llalal said them, as if they were a password of some sort.

"True enough," said Jim. It was the only thing he could think of to say. Llalal let go of his arm with a gesture almost of disappointment.

"Nonetheless, Brother," he said quietly. "All of the Maureg inns, except those down by the waterfront in this city, are full of Walats. You'd be best off staying overnight among your own people; even though you are plainly . . ." he hesitated, "strangers, and from some far island."

"Thanks," said Jim. "We'll see." He left the boat thoughtfully.

Once upon the quay, however, and out of earshot not only of Llalal, but of any other Mauregs, he told the others of the conversation.

". . . And what I think, after hearing Llalal say we're plainly strangers," he wound up, "is that any place but an inn full of Mauregs is the best place for us. We may look just like them, but the real Mauregs seem to sense a difference when they have too much to do with us at close quarters. I think we're safest among the other two races, myself. What do the rest of you think?"

"I think we're in trouble among *any* Aliens!"

grumbled Curt. "After all, if that Alien spaceship hadn't broken down and stranded us here—"

"Well, I think Jim's right about the Mauregs sensing we're different," said Ellen, unexpectedly. "We may move and talk and dress like Mauregs, but our attitudes and opinions are human and they feel the difference. Where else could we stay besides a waterfront inn, Peep?"

"There is a Walat-operated inn right by the aardart pens," said Peep. "And the aardarts are a form of riding animal we will have to hire to ride across to Joffo, the trader's port on the other side of this rather large island of Hekko. Shall we go there?"

They did. The inn, when they got to it, was very similar to the one in which Llalal had been staying in Chyk, except that the ceilings were higher, and the tables and benches in the common room on the ground floor were bigger. They had come in on the evening tide and night had fallen by the time they reached the inn. A female Walat lighted them upstairs to their rooms, which were wide and clean, but except for the strips of carpet used for sitting and sleeping, without furniture. The rooms were on the second floor, and as the landlady left them, there drifted up from the common room below the voice of an apparently drunken, male Walat, trying to sing some kind of song.

"I didn't know they had wine or anything like that," said Curt.

"It has not been alcohol that has brought the individual downstairs to such a state," said Peep, "although alcoholic drinks are not unknown on Quebahr. It is a local plant, the sap of which has a particularly strong effect on Walats. Our singer is, in effect, drugged."

"I should think . . . oh!" said Ellen. "Did that landlady or whatever she was leave? There was something I wanted to ask her." She hurried out into the darkened second-floor corridor.

"I'd better follow and make sure she doesn't become lost," said Peep. He trotted after Ellen. Jim and Curt started after them, then gave it up, took off their weapons and sat down by the lamp that the landlady had left them. They began to discuss getting the ends of their quarterstaves capped with metal before leaving Hekko Port for Joffo.

They were still at this when Ellen burst back into the room.

"Quick, Jim!" she said. "It's Peep! That drugged Walat's trying to make him do bundii tricks downstairs. Peep's in trouble!"

8

Both Jim and Curt jumped to their feet. But Jim shook his head and pushed Curt back as the tall young man started to follow him.

"Stay with Ellen!" Jim snapped, and started off at a run. Halfway down the stairs, he suddenly remembered he had left his quarterstaff back in the room, but sounds of smashing furniture and crockery were coming from downstairs with the bellowing of a Walat voice. The drugged customer had evidently gone berserk. There was no time to go back for the quarterstaff now. Jim leaped on down, rounded the turn in the stairs and landed at ground level, by the kitchen entrance of the common room. The landlady was watching from this entrance and shivering with fury.

"Stay back, O Friend!" she said angrily between her teeth to Jim. "We've sent for the Night Guard. They'll shorten his tail for him, the drugged plains animal! To have this happen in my inn! Next week my husband's uncle arrives and I'll see that one of his cousins is left to guard our premises from back-country devils like this! Where are you going, Maureg?"

"He's got our bundii." Jim was peering into the darkness of the common room. All the lamps in it had been smashed and dimly, by what light filtered through a starlit gap of window, Jim could see the drugged Walat staggering around, his enormous long sword glittering as he swung blindly at everything around him.

"Your bundii ran into the food-storage cellar, beyond," said the landlady. "The drugged one didn't see it. Your pet'll be safe there until the Night Guard arrive—oh!"

The last exclamation was caused by the drugged Walat's whoop of triumph as he discovered the cellar entrance the landlady had just pointed out.

"Bundii!" he roared. "I'll make you jump, bundii!" he roared, and plunged through. Jim left the foot of the stairs and ran after him.

"Little Maureg! What're you doing?" he heard the land-lady cry behind him as he stumbled over a shattered bench and dived for the doorway of the cellar. "You can't do anything! He'll kill you!"

But Jim was already on the steps to the cellar. He

stumbled, half falling in the dark, and ended up suddenly on hard-packed earth, surrounded by the dry odor of native vegetables. The cellar was utterly dark and still.

"Peep?" he said, hesitantly. Suddenly there was a roar, and a huge body flung past him, smashing into what sounded like a rack of laden shelves. Jim dodged and blinked. His eyes were beginning to adjust, and he saw that a small window high in one wall let in a feeble amount of starlight.

"Dear me," said the concerned voice of Peep in English, from somewhere in the darkness, "is that you, young friend?"

"Jim," Jim identified himself, also in English. "Ellen came—" He sensed rather than saw a towering blackness in the dark cellar, throwing itself at him, and dodged instinctively. Another set of shelves went crashing behind him.

"No y'don't—" muttered the voice of the Walat thickly. "Talk'n two voice not going t'help you. C'mere, you—whoever y'are, 'n I'll split y'r gizzard. . . ." This was followed by hoarse breathing in the darkness.

"Do not speak, young friend," said Peep, clearly. "He will attack any voice. For myself this does not matter—"

There was a roar from the Walat, another charge and crash.

"—It is," continued the voice of Peep, a little

breathlessly in English, "an excellent opportunity for me to practice remaining nonviolent—"

"Got you!" roared the Walat, triumphantly. There was another crash. Jim had found a corner. He crowded back into it.

"—under," continued Peep's voice, but with a slight note of irritation, "extreme—"

Crash! went another set of shelves.

"—ly trying—"

Crash!

"Circumstances. *Skevamp!*" said Peep. "Be calm, young friend, as I—"

Crash!

"Bulg? Har y nnyn rakks—I beg your pardon, young friend, for these slight expostulations, but—"

"Take that!" roared the Walat. Half the cellar seemed to come crashing to the floor and roll around the room like continuing thunder.

"Brrrr jha ykk nppotlittt! Cha ylll mttn gar—" There was a series of meaty thuds, followed by a sudden and nerve-racking silence.

"Oh, no . . ." came the unhappy voice of Peep. "What have I done? Speak to me, my poor Walat friend, I implore you. Please speak to me! Young friend . . . Jim . . . where are you? Find a light. I fear that in my usual intemperate fashion I've—"

"Shhh!" hissed Jim. "Somebody's coming. Don't talk!"

Light suddenly struck into the cellar from above. Blinking in the abrupt glare, Jim saw the big body of the Walat lying on its back only a few feet from his corner and Peep standing over it with his paws clasped together. He was the perfect picture of an Atakit riven by remorse. He was also, thought Jim gratefully, the perfect picture of a timid bundii riven by terror. Hastily Jim stepped over to him and took him by one hand.

"There, there, bundii . . ." said Jim, soothingly, but with an undertone of warning in his voice that he hoped Peep would notice even through his emotion. "I'll take you upstairs now."

He turned toward the cellar stairs, and stopped.

At the top stood the landlady and two Walats wearing armbands and carrying long poles with maceheads on their top ends. The landlady was carrying the lamp that was illuminating the cellar, and the two Walats were armed to the teeth. But they were all merely standing and staring at Jim.

Their eyes went from Jim to the fallen figure of the drugged Walat, who was now beginning to stir and mutter his way up out of unconsciousness. Then their eyes went incredulously back to Jim again. None of them bothered to look at Peep.

"Uh—come along, bundii," said Jim, leading Peep by the hand up the stairs. At the top of the stairs the three Walats made way for him. As he passed, the landlady bowed and the two Night Guards, or whatever they were, saluted.

"Good night," said Jim, and bolted for his room upstairs, with Peep following close behind him.

"All my fault! It was all my fault!" said Peep unhappily, when at last they got safely back to their rooms where Curt and Ellen had faithfully waited through it all. Jim explained the matter to them.

"But it wasn't your fault at all, Peep," said Jim. "The Walat picked on you, not the other way around. Let's get some sleep and forget it. It's all over now, anyway."

But Jim discovered, when they got up the next morning and left the inn, that it wasn't. When they paid their bill, the landlady came as close to simpering as a Walat was able to, and the street before the inn was full of Walats who stared incredulously at Jim as the four of them left for the aardart pens.

"What's wrong with them all?" growled Jim, embarrassed as they finally left the crowd behind and turned a corner toward the pens.

"They think it was *you* who defeated the Walat, and courage and battle prowess are large items in the Walat scale of values, young friend," sighed Peep. He brightened. "Of course, in a way they are giving you no less than your due, for it required a high order of courage for you to charge into that cellar."

"I just wasn't thinking," said Jim, his ears burning in the old familiar style. "Forget it, shall we?"

Except that the noises and odors were different, the aardart pens were very much like the pens full of beef cattle waiting rail shipment Jim had seen on a vacation trip in Texas two years before. The aardarts themselves were something like dun-colored, heavy-bodied giraffes—about the same size, but differently proportioned with thicker legs and shorter necks.

Their hind legs, like those of a giraffe, were shorter than the front pair. When they galloped, this gave them the rocking-horse gait peculiar to giraffes in a hurry. Their voice was either a deep grunt, or a high-pitched scream that was somewhat unnerving to the three humans until they got used to it. The aardarts smelled pleasantly like the wild clover of Earth.

Prices were posted, and so the usual dickering was avoided. Jim contracted for four beasts and saddles and the Walat in charge produced a small ladder by which they mounted the animals one by one. All went well until Peep climbed last of all onto his mount.

It abruptly sat down, and Peep slid off. The aardart stood up again.

"What's wrong with you?" bellowed the Walat to the animal, slapping it on the nose.

"Never mind," said Jim hastily. It had suddenly come to him what the trouble was. The fourth animal had been loaded with the pack gear, food, and drink they would need for the two-day overland trip. The Walat had assumed that Peep would simply ride on top of the pack, like any pet bundii. The only difficulty with this was that Peep was not a bundii—weighing perhaps a hundred pounds, Earth-and-Quebahrian weight. He was an Atakit from the heavy-gravity world of Juseleminopratipup with about eight hundred pounds packed into his pint-sized body. This, plus the pack, had been too much for the aardart, and it had protested in the immemorial fashion of over-loaded pack animals.

Of course, there was no explaining this to the Walat.

"Our bundii may have scratched him getting on," said Jim. "We'll just let the bundii run alongside for the first hour or so. He needs the exercise anyway."

"O Maureg!" protested the Walat, "you've got to show these aardarts who's in control or you'll never stop having trouble with them."

"Run! Run!" squeaked Peep anxiously, bundii-fashion. His eyes had reddened slightly when he had seen the Walat slap the aardart's nose. Another slap and Peep's nonviolence might give way before his sense of outrage. In broad daylight this could be disastrous to their masquerade.

"See there," said Jim, hastily. "The bundii wants his morning run. It's settled." And so, with Peep trotting alongside, leaving the disgusted Walat pen-master behind, off they went.

As soon as they were out of sight of the pens, over the horizon of the brown-grassed plain that seemed to stretch forever, they stopped, unpacked the portable ladder from among their supplies, and helped Peep up on their stoutest aardart. This one did not sit down, though it looked back over its shoulder and grunted in protest. Ellen insisted on being the one to ride the pack animal. As she pointed out, she was the lightest, and the saddles were no more comfortable than the pack on which she would be riding.

All this settled, they started up again. Their aardarts refused obstinately to approach anything like a gallop. They could be prevailed upon, however, to trot. And their trot, with two legs on the same side moving forward at a time, was nowhere near as joggling as a horse's trot. So they trotted on, sending up a trail of dust in the sunlight at their backs.

On these unmarked plains the Walats, who were native to them, had an instinctive sense of direction. Humans did not—but then, luckily, neither did Mauregs. Consequently, the pen-master had given them aardarts born in the pen at Joffo, the trader-town that was their destination, for the aardarts had a homing instinct. A trained rider, or the need for food or water, could move them in other directions than homeward, but they returned to their birthing area when given their heads.

The advantage of this became more apparent when the trail dwindled and finally disappeared in an endless sea of the waving brown grass, which seemed alive with singing insects, the first real birdlike flying creatures they had seen, and occasional small, bounding animals. The Walats who normally crossed these plains seldom did so in a straight line, Peep remarked.

"Usually they are driving their own private herds of aardarts," said Peep. He had recovered his usual sunny good spirits on discovering that the aardart under him was no longer protesting about his weight.

"What do they want so many aardarts for that they make up herds of them?" asked Curt. "Do they change mounts every half hour, or what?"

"No, young friend," said Peep. "The aardarts are a source of food to them as well as a source of mounts. In earlier times, when the Walats were mainly nomads, the aardarts represented the only visible form of wealth. Even today, on the plains here, a Walat is measured by his herd. We should be seeing some soon."

In fact, they soon did. Shortly after noon they passed a large herd of aardarts being driven by mounted Walats, cowboy fashion. An hour or so later they passed another, smaller herd. Shortly after that, however, they were themselves overtaken by a large Walat on a tall, lean aardart.

Ellen was the first to spot him.

"Look behind!" she called suddenly, and they all turned around in their saddles.

When they first saw the rider, he seemed to be making no progress at all. He and his aardart appeared only to be bouncing up and down in the brown sea of grass. But as the rider drew closer, Jim saw that he was making easily three times the speed of their own trotting beasts, and that he was wearing two heavy pouches slung over his shoulders.

"A mail carrier," explained Peep.

He came on without pausing, the rocking-horse motion of his galloping animal becoming more and more apparent, and passed within a few yards of them.

"O Maureg!" he shouted across to Jim as he passed, "you don't look very big to be beating up drugged ones!" Coughing with laughter, he slapped the side of his aardart, waved cheerfully, and rode on. They watched him dwindle, hull-down, so to speak, on the brown horizon ahead.

Jim scowled.

"What's the trouble?" asked Curt.

"The trouble," said Jim, "is the business of our being identified this way. Evidently, because of what happened back at the inn, they'll be recognizing us wherever we go."

"What puzzles me," put in Ellen, thoughtfully, "is why the Walats are so ready to believe you could have beaten up one of them—even one who was drugged. It would be like a ten-year-old boy beating *you* up. I should think they'd be more ready to believe there was some accident involved in what happened—like the drugged Walat falling over something in the dark and knocking himself out."

"There've been a lot of funny things happening—" Jim checked himself, on the verge of sharing his suspicions that a group of Federation Aliens were out to get them into trouble, if not to kill them outright. He still had no proof of any kind. He told himself the others would not believe him, that was all. "Maybe you're right," he said.

"We ought to keep Jim out of sight as much as

possible if we run into any other Walats,'' Ellen told the others. She sounded worried. She was, thought Jim, really as bad as Peep where it came to a chance of anyone or anything getting hurt. He let the others talk about how they might disguise him or make him inconspicuous and returned to his own thoughts.

Something had been sticking in the back of his mind like a sandbur, nagging at him. It was the odd phrase that Llalal had spoken to him on parting— how had it gone? Something about you couldn't see into a mountain but neither could anyone see to the bottom of the sea. The more he thought about it, the more sure he was that it was some kind of fraternal password or challenge which had called for an equally formal answer. It was just too odd and flowery a phrase to make sense otherwise.

If that was so, it raised two questions. First, to what sort of outfit did that password belong? And, second, what had made Llalal think he was a member of the outfit? Jim found himself wishing he had stopped and questioned Llalal bluntly about it. Even if, as was almost certain, the shipowner had refused to answer, Jim might have been able to learn something more by the way the Maureg refused. Jim's mind went on, worrying the problem as a dog worries a bone, in the habit it had built up over the last few years of study and work . . .

Jim started out of his thoughts, suddenly. He was aware that he had just been asked some kind of question. He looked around and saw the other three staring at him expectantly.

"What?" he said. "Oh, sorry—I wasn't listening."

"We want to know what you think," said Ellen, "about wrapping your right hand in a bandage. We can say you had it stepped on by an aardart, and since it's your sword hand as far as any of these Walats will know, you can't fight anybody until it heals. What about it, Jim? Isn't that a good idea?"

"Oh, we don't need to do that," growled Jim, feeling self-conscious.

"I think it may be a very good idea, indeed, young friend," said Peep, seriously, "these Walats are unfortunate victims of a historical cult of violence. Champions among them are constantly being challenged, and a Maureg who has won a fight with a Walat is bound to be challenged."

Curt and Ellen agreed. After some little argument, Jim gave in. Ellen did an impressive job of binding him up and they continued on their way as the sun dipped toward the horizon ahead of them.

As sunset flooded the brown landscape, turning it a rusty color, they saw smoke off to their left and shortly came level to the point where they could see they were passing some fairly good-sized encampment about a quarter mile to their left.

"Better stay clear of them, don't you think?" Jim asked. "And camp for the night by ourselves, someplace up ahead?"

"We may not have the chance, young friends,"

said Peep. A single rider was galloping in their direction from the encampment.

"You mean he might invite us to stay with them? Can't we just say no if he does?"

"Not without insulting them," answered Peep worriedly. "The Walats out on these plains are supposed to be very different from those we have met so far in the cities. Out here they are less civilized and follow ancient rules of hospitality, honor, and clan authority. We've a full day's ride tomorrow before we're back in the civilization of the traders' port on the other side of the island. It would be best not to make enemies."

They reined their aardarts to a halt and waited. The rider, a young Walat, came galloping up and circled them at full gallop before heading back. He did not pause at all, but as he circled them, he shouted.

"O Mauregs, the Clan Siakin offers you fire and food. In the name of Siakin, Clan Chief, you are welcome!"

"Tell him you are grateful, young friend," muttered Peep to Jim.

"We are grateful!" shouted Jim. The rider flung up an arm in acknowledgment, completed his circle, and still at headlong gallop, headed back toward the encampment.

At their more sedate trot, the three humans and Peep followed. When they reached the outskirts of the encampment, they found it laid out in a series of circles within circles. The outer circle was the tethered aardarts. Within this were family carpets under awnings, and then a zone almost exclusively occupied by full-grown male Walats, and within this final zone was an open area with a huge fire at its center. A tent with an elevated chair or throne in front of it faced the fire.

As soon as they reached the outer circle, a bevy of large female Walats swarmed about them, assisting them to dismount, tethering their aardarts, pitching awnings, and building a cooking fire for them. The din of grunting or screaming animals and shouting, deep-voiced Walats made Jim's head spin. In all that noise it was quite easy to speak openly to Peep in English and have him answer without danger of giving away his bundii disguise. The very publicness of the encampment made it private.

"What're they going to expect of us?" Jim asked the Atakit.

"I'm afraid I can't tell you, young friend," Peep confessed. "The briefing device failed to inform me what to expect if we should be invited guests of a clan of plains Walats. Evidently such a happening was not imagined by those who fed the briefing device."

"You think this is all because of that business with the drugged Walat back at the inn?"

"I cannot think what else. Perhaps—" Peep's voice broke into its bundii squeak. "Walat! Walat!"

Peep's gaze was going over Jim's shoulder. Jim

turned about and saw looming over him a tall Walat loaded with weapons.

"O mighty Maureg?" boomed the Walat, coughing with cheerful laughter. "There's no sap around the encampment, so I haven't been able to get myself drugged up; but how about a little bout with the swords, anyway, just to show us country folks how you do it?"

9

Staring grimly at the Walat, Jim lifted his bandaged right hand into the firelight.

"Sorry," said Jim. "My aardart stepped on it earlier today."

For a moment the Walat said nothing, but merely stood there.

"Your aardart stepped on it," he said, finally. It was impossible for Jim to tell by the Walat's tone of voice whether he was jeering, or not.

"That's right." Jim scowled.

"And that means you cannot fight me?"

"That's just what it means," growled Jim. He was beginning to feel stubborn. Come to think of it, he thought, why did I have to bandage up that hand? If I don't want to fight, I don't want to fight."

"O Maureg," said the Walat, softly, "there was a mail rider that came by here and told us of a Maureg who, with no weapons but his hands, outfought a drugged one of my race. I see now we should have asked that mail rider if such Mauregs were likely to have their sword hands stepped on by aardarts. We had hoped to welcome one with courage to our fires and are disappointed. But it is not all lost, for at least we have given shelter to a cripple."

"So you have," said Jim, firmly and almost cheerfully.

The Walat stayed looking at him for a moment more.

"But cripples should be grateful, and therefore polite," said the Walat. "And I see you have not bowed to me as an inferior should. Therefore, perhaps I should teach you better manners—"

"Just a minute!"

It was Curt's voice. Jim turned to stare at him in time to see Curt scramble up from a seated position, dragging the two quarterstaves with him. As he uncoiled to his full height, which was equal to that of the Walat, the Walat's eyes opened slightly.

"I'll fight you," said Curt. In the firelight Jim saw that Curt's face was pale and his forehead shining slightly with sweat. Even his voice trembled slightly, but he stood facing the Walat. "With these!" Curt said, lifting the staves to show the Walat.

"Curt!" Jim said in English. "Are you crazy?"

Curt ignored him. The Walat looked at the staves and then back at Curt.

"You wish to fight me?" he said, "and with these little sticks?"

"That's right!" said Curt. "My friend can't, but since you've come here throwing your weight around, I'll fight you instead—"

"Curt! You know you aren't even a match for *me!*" said Jim, beginning to sweat also. He had suspected the truth about Curt before this—the tall young man was prone to worries and fears that did not seem to work on Jim the same way; and since Curt was ashamed of these, he was always trying to prove his courage. He was like a man in deathly fear of heights who doggedly sets out to learn mountain climbing.

"Shut up!" snapped Curt out of the corner of his mouth, also in English, "you're valuable to us, and I'm not. Don't you see he was going to make you fight anyway?"

"He couldn't have—" But Jim did not get a chance to finish. With a coughing laugh, the Walat swept one of the sticks out of Curt's hand.

"Sticks, then!" he boomed. "Come on." Turning abruptly, he stalked away, and Curt went after him.

"Hold on!" shouted Jim, and started to follow, but found a horde of Walats of all sizes crowding in the way, eager to follow also. Growing furious, Jim shoved his way through. The youngsters, the women, made way for him, but he was slowed down, and as he got closer to where the leaping flames of the huge fire in the center of the camp showed flickering tips above the heads of the crowd, he came finally against a barrier.

The barrier was the close-packed bodies of male Walats, two and three deep, ranked around the open space by the fire to watch the entertainment of Curt fighting the Walat challenger.

"Let me through!" snarled Jim, now fighting mad himself. But the two- and three-hundred-pound males ignored him. He was like a child trying to move grownups.

He backed up a step to charge into their ranks, but just then a small shadow slipped ahead of him.

"Allow me, young friend," whispered the voice of Peep in English, and the next second the four or five large Walats in front of Jim flew aside as if struck by a battering ram. They went sprawling with roars of astonishment and fury.

Jim charged through the gap. Peep innocently followed, but Jim had no time to keep track of the Atakit. He spotted Curt and the Walat squared off with quarterstaves in front of the fire. Jim ran up to them and wrenched the quarterstaff out of Curt's hand.

"If there's any fighting to be done," he said, loudly in the native tongue, "I'll do it!!"

"What makes you think you can do it any better than I can?" shouted Curt. He was as pale as the snow scene on a Christmas card, but his jaw was determined.

"Because I'm not scared the way you are, you idiot!" muttered Jim, under his breath to the other young man. "And because I'm better with this stick, and you know it!"

Curt went rigid. Jim stood glaring at him.

"Well," coughed the Walat who had challenged Jim in the first place. "Which one is it going to be? It's going to be one of you, because when I get geared up for a fight—"

"When Bratig gets geared up for a fight," interrupted a harsh voice off to their right, "he waits and finds out whether his Clan Chief agrees he should fight. Doesn't he, Bratig?"

Bratig shrank visibly. He, Curt and Jim all turned to see an ancient Walat being assisted by two young males up onto the elevated seat before the tent. The old Walat had been huge once, judging by his bony frame, but his body had fallen away to nothing more than wrinkled skin and sparse flesh. His eyes in the grizzled fur of his face were like dark burns in a rug, and his body hair had gone almost colorless with age.

"What is all this fuss involving my guests? What is it?" crackled the old Walat, once he was settled on his throne. "No, not you, Bratig—let someone else tell me." A babble burst from the bystanders, many of whom, it now appeared, had been in the vicinity of the humans' campfire when Bratig had come to challenge Jim.

"Quiet! That's enough!" roared the old Walat finally, and the clamor fell silent. "Bratig, come closer to me, here."

Bratig came slowly forward.

"Who am I, Bratig?"

"Siakin," answered Bratig, sullenly.

"Siakin, *and* Clan Siakin!" snapped the old Walat. "I am Chief of the Clan and the Clan is I. Is it not so, people of Clan Siakin?" He lifted his head to look out at the crowd.

"It is so— It is so!" The sound of the answer from the surrounding crowd rose like the muttering thunder of a wave on the shore and died out as a wave dies off farther down the beach.

"These Mauregs are the guests of Clan Siakin—my guests. And I am told, Bratig, that when one of them said he was not able to fight, you began to insult him, so that his friend was forced to challenge you in his place. This happened by one of my fires—to my guests. Are they not my guests?" He lifted his head again.

"Your guests, O Siakin—your guests!" rolled and muttered the response of the crowd.

"When did a guest at my fires have to fight, even if he did not wish sport—let alone being hurt and crippled for it?" asked Siakin, lowering his head and addressing the question this time to Bratig. Bratig did not answer.

"Leave my fires, Bratig," said the Clan Chief. "I send you away from them for three seasons. Go into the cities and live with the lawless, clanless Walats that sleep under stone roofs and work for the little Noifs. If you find their way, a way without law and guest-right, better than the life of the Clan, stay with them. But if there is good in you, come back at the end of the time, and you can sit at our fires again. Now *leave!*"

The last word came out like the snap of a bow-string. Bratig turned and went into a crowd that parted to let him through. Siakin struggled to his feet and the young males on either side of him moved forward to help him up. With their aid he came down from the platform and stood facing Curt, Jim, and Peep. Even bent and shrunken with age, the Walat Chief was nearly half a foot taller than Curt.

"When you go back to your people," Siakin said wearily, "tell them it was not always like this. Now Mauregs like yourselves cheat us, and clever little Noifs make machines to destroy us. But once on these plains we held by the old customs. You have talked to Siakin, who remembers the days when this was so. Remember that, O Mauregs, when you see some clanless Walat wallowing in the stink of the cities."

Siakin turned away toward his tent. Jim, Curt, and Peep turned in the other direction and slowly they made their way back to their own fire and posses-sions through a crowd that made way for them as they went.

They got back to their own area and sat down. Jim

had been following close behind Curt, who had led the way back. Now, as he and Curt sat down, he saw that Ellen and Peep had unaccountably lagged behind. He looked at Curt. Curt had his eyes lowered, examining a bowl of food he had picked up.

Jim reached over and shoved the quarterstaves away among the luggage. He looked back at Curt, scowling.

"Look," he said, and even to his own ears his voice sounded harsh and uncomfortable, "what I said out there—I said the first thing that came into my head that I thought would work. I didn't care how I stopped you, just so I stopped you—"

"No," said Curt, quickly, but still looking down at the bowl. "You were right. I was scared. I always am—I just thought I could do something in spite of it, for once." He drew a quick breath, then looked up and around without meeting Jim's eye. "Where are Ellen and Peep? Oh, here they come, now."

"Yeah," said Jim. "I guess we beat them back here."

Peep and Ellen came up and sat down. Suddenly they were all (except Peep) talking at once. About Siakin, about the Walats of the plains, and the camp about them, about anything and everything—except the little period of time beginning when Bratig had showed up to challenge Jim and ending when the Walat had knuckled under to his Clan Chief.

Gradually, the pace of the chatter slowed down, but none of them ate a great deal, and Curt was the first finished. He rolled up in his cape, saying he was more tired than he had been since the first day when they had walked down the side of the volcano.

Looking across the fire at Ellen and Peep, Jim saw them watching him sympathetically.

"Think I'll turn in, too," he grunted and, turning away from the fire, rolled up in his own cape. Gradually the Walat camp quieted down into slumber around them, but Jim lay awake for a long time, watching the unfamiliar stars.

It was a rough life, he thought to himself at last, finally drifting off into sleep. A rough life, in a rough world. He was just enough awake to correct himself on that—in a rough universe.

They woke at dawn and got going early the next day. By midafternoon they were able to see the dark line of Joffo on the horizon; but it was late afternoon before they had reached the traders' port, released their aardarts to the pen-master there, and found rooms in an inn overlooking the Joffo waterfront.

"It's different here than in any city we've been in so far on Quebahr," said Ellen, leaning out an unglazed window of their second-story rooms to listen to the babble of the waterfront below, noisy with peddlers and the fierce arguments of traders and shippers. "Shouldn't you tell us something about it, Peep?"

"The difference lies principally in the equal division of races here in this port," Peep replied. "Normally, one particular race dominates a city or an area. For example, the island on which we landed was Maureg territory; Hekko Island, except for Joffo, is occupied principally by Walats. And, as you know, Annohne, our ultimate destination, belongs to the Noifs.''

"There hasn't been any pattern of conquest then—one race dominating and taking over the lands of the others—the way there's been on Earth?'' Curt asked the question rather soberly. Some of his exuberance seemed to have been left behind for good in the Walat camp of Clan Siakin.

"Exactly, young friend!'' Peep beamed approvingly, lifting his small black nose to Curt. "And this situation can be explained historically. Unlike Earth, with its continental masses, Quebahr has only its clusters of islands, with large ocean distances between the clusters. On Quebahr the three intelligent races developed into primitive civilized states independently, on separated island clusters, and without a knowledge of each other's existence. Of course, they developed at different rates, but they had all reached roughly the same cultural level by the time the development of large sailing craft made movement between the island clusters possible. When they came into contact, all three races were so equal that one could not dominate or exterminate the others. Moreover, their cultural inclinations fitted together—artisanship to the Mauregs, police work to the Walats, science and administration to the Noifs. Thus there is a balance that causes them to live together essentially in peace.''

"Civil, military, and administrative-technical . . ." mused Ellen, thoughtfully. "It *is* a balance."

"It's kind of a fine balance, though—don't you think?" asked Curt.

"I think," answered Ellen, "that it's been in better balance than it's in now. That it struck a balance some time back, but as this world becomes more modern, the development of one of the races is likely to affect the general social structure unequally. Not to mention the fact that the development of one race may be misunderstood by another and resented. Do you remember Siakin, and his bitterness about the present, compared to the good old days of the Walats?"

"You may be right, young friend," Peep said to her. "Though, as a world, Quebahr is still pretty backward and violent, even now. And any culture— particularly a three-race culture like this one—that is essentially violent, is essentially uneasy. And its uneasiness, which may be compared to the ocean's choppiness on a slightly breezy day, may often be mistaken for the onset of a large storm, or even the major disturbance of the sea caused by an underwater earthquake, or—"

"Excuse me, Peep," interrupted Jim, "but how about getting down to practical matters? There's still an hour or so of daylight left, and we want to get a ship to Annohne as soon as we can—tomorrow, if possible. Now, you started to tell us what we needed to know about Joffo, and then you got off on geography and cultural developments."

"Dear me," said Peep, contritely, punching his brow in his usual sledge-hammer fashion, "so I did. Forgive me. What I started to say is that, being a traders' port, with the three races all about equally represented among the shipowners here, we can choose pretty freely among the ships bound for Annohne to find the one on which we wish to travel. Now I would suggest, since we wish to avoid attracting the attention of the most scientific-minded of the local races as long as possible, that we do not arrange passage on any Noif vessel, where we would be thrown into prolonged contact with one or more members of that intellectually curious race. It may be they would suspect nothing, but why take chances, since the briefing I was given on this world has proved inadequate on occasions before this?"

"Right," said Curt. "No Noif ships."

"Or Maureg," put in Jim. "The Mauregs may not know we aren't Mauregs, but remember Llalal certainly sensed a difference about us. I think the less we have to do with Mauregs the better."

"That leaves Walats," said Ellen.

"Check," said Jim. "And I'd just as soon not have any more challenges from Walats. If we go in a group, the three of us with Peep, they're sure to recognize us."

He stopped and glanced at Peep, who nodded.

"Quite true," said Peep. "Three Mauregs and a bundii, and one of the Mauregs having such-and-so characteristics that correspond with your appearance—

that is no doubt how we are identified in common gossip. It would be well if we split up in public, to remove the primary identification, that of four individuals, together.''

"So," said Jim, "why don't Ellen and you, Curt, go out and arrange passage to Annohne with some Walat skipper? Peep and I will stay put here—better yet," he added, inspiration kindling within him, "I'll go with Peep back up into town and see about getting those metal caps for our quarterstaves. As they are, the quarterstaves are useful clubs, but with the metal caps on their ends they'll be actual weapons.''

It was settled. Curt and Ellen left the inn for the docks, while Jim and Peep headed in toward the center of the town to find a smithy. They located one only three streets from the inn, and the smith, a Walat, promised to have the staves shod before sailing time on the outgoing tide the following morning.

So it happened that Jim and Peep returned to their rooms within half an hour of leaving them. Surprisingly, as they came up the stairs to the second story of the inn, on which their rooms were located, they heard voices.

"Don't tell me," said Jim to Peep, as they reached the top of the stairs, "that Curt and Ellen got passage arranged for us so soon.''

They stepped into the room. There were two people who turned to face them as they entered. But the two were not Curt and Ellen. They were Maureg men.

"Brother," said one to Jim, "we meet again."

It was Llalal. Jim stared at the Maureg incredulously.

"How did you get here?" Jim asked. "I thought it was faster across the island than anyone could sail around it."

"The Noifs," answered Llalal, "have ships that travel without sails, and in the night as well as the day. I was here before you and I have brought a friend to meet you. For just as I use the Noif's ship to help defeat the Noif, so we have a duty to lay upon you—stranger, whoever you may be, and from whatever strange place you come."

10

For a moment Jim did not move, and a cold stillness woke inside him and seemed to spread out through his body into his legs and arms. He remembered the voice aboard the lifeboat telling them that the lives of castaways on Quebahr were considered less important to the Alien Federation than the preservation of Quebahr's ignorance about the Federation. If Llalal had recognized them as beings from another world, then the fat was in the fire.

Then his courage came back with a swoop. Well, he thought, at least we can start out by denying everything.

"What do you mean—duty?" demanded Jim. "And what's this about coming from some far place?"

"You are different," said Llalal. "So different

that you could only have come from some far island cluster to which none of us has ever been. You travel with some purpose none of us understands. You play a strange sport with sticks among yourselves that no one has ever seen before. And you are strong enough to defeat a Walat barehanded without receiving a mark upon you.''

Jim's hopes began to lift. To be taken for strangers from some unknown island cluster was bad enough, for it suggested that the Mauregs, at least, had been more conscious of differences in them than they had suspected. But it was at least better than being identified for the otherworldly characters they really were.

''You don't want to believe everything you hear,'' he said cautiously. ''That Walat was drugged . . .''

''That we know,'' said the unidentified Maureg with Llalal. ''Also we know what it is to see with our foreheads in the dark, which no Noif or Walat can really appreciate.'' Sudden understanding flooded Jim's mind. Here was the answer to Ellen's question about the easy belief of the Walat watchmen and landlady in his ability to conquer someone twice his weight and strength. Of course, they had assumed that his Maureg sonar had given him the advantage in the dark. That was probably why Bratig had led Curt into the central area of the camp, where the firelight would cancel out the advantage Bratig assumed Curt's forehead bumps would give him in the dimness and tricky shadows about the cooking fires, in the outer zones of the camp.

"Still," said Llalal, "to do what you did required strength far above what any Maureg man might expect to have. And we need the strength. We need whatever other strange abilities or skills you, or your friends, or"—he gestured to Peep—"this bundii that talks to you in a strange language and acts more like a man than a bundii—may have."

Jim shook his head.

"Sorry," he said. "We've got private business of our own to take care of."

"Listen," said Llalal, eagerly leaning forward, "from here you go to Annohne—"

"Who says so?" snapped Jim.

"Even now, your companions arrange for passage. From the time you passed through the village on the volcano's side," said Llalal, "you have been watched. Where you came from before that, we have not been able to trace. But from the moment you passed through the village on the slope of the volcano, we know almost every step you've taken. I was in Chyk when the word came to me by runner ahead of you, that strangers, *from higher on the volcano,* had passed through that village and glimpsed one of the spring-guns our people have made after the Noif design. I went to the harbor master's office to see you for myself."

He paused, looking at Jim.

"For a while I even thought that you might be one of us, for our brotherhood is spread over many islands and there could be some members I don't know. But I spoke the Brotherhood words to you as you were leaving the ship at Hekko Port.'' Llalal stared at Jim. ''But you did not answer, *'but the sea is larger than the mountain and hides more,'* as you should have done if you'd been one of us. So we do not know you, but we know you are Mauregs, and so we have a right to ask your help.''

''You'll have to take my word for it,'' said Jim. ''We can't help you. We couldn't if we wanted to.''

''How can you say that—you, a Maureg?'' burst out Llalal's companion. ''Can't you see what's happening on all the islands? In our grandfather's time, even, it was all level between us, the way the Triple Gods designed us. To the Walat, strength; to the Noif, wisdom; to the Maureg, the seeing-in-the-dark. From the beginning, there was this balance. But now the Noif threatens us, Maureg and Walat alike. Though the Walats will not see the danger.''

''Maybe you're exaggerating it,'' said Jim, watching them closely.

''Exaggerate!'' said the other Maureg. ''This isn't a matter of spring-guns we can copy! It's not a matter of ships-without-sails! The weapon in the temple at Annohne will sweep the world clear of the Walats and ourselves. It is a weapon only the Noifs can work. We have built an exact copy and it will not kill for us. Moreover, it is a weapon that will slay one race among a crowd and leave those of another race unharmed.''

Jim blinked.

"Ha'n ay!" he said, as automatically as he had said it to Peep the first day on Quebahr when none of the humans yet realized they could speak the local language. "You're kidding me!"

Llalal almost pounced into the middle of the conversation.

"You did not know this!" he burst out triumphantly. "I *thought* you did not know of it! It was because you did not know that you were unwilling to work with us. Isn't it so?"

"Wait. Hold on . . ." Jim scowled. "How do you know the Noifs have a weapon like that? You can't believe all you hear . . ."

"Hear!" cried the other Maureg. "Our own people have crept into the temple and seen criminals cut down by the machine! It's true that at the moment it kills only Noifs and leaves Walats and our own people unharmed. But we have talked to our own people imprisoned in the temple and they say the Noifs are sure to make it finally kill Maureg and Walat, while leaving the Noifs themselves untouched."

"They've seen it work? Your—our people?" said Jim. "It must be a trick."

"Why should it be a trick, when they didn't know we were watching?" asked Llalal. "We went in through the caves of Annohne mountain, and tunneled into the air vents of the temple. No one but a Maureg could follow such a route without getting lost. We saw the weapon work."

"I'll bet you saw something faked up," grunted

Jim. "You saw Maureg or Walat prisoners that'd been poisoned or something and healthy Noifs that weren't affected by whatever blanket discharge hit them." He felt the same old stubbornness rising inside himself that had risen when he had argued with Ward Stuyler about odds. A physical weapon that killed in the hands of one race but didn't in the hands of another was physically impossible.

"But it wasn't Maureg and Walats we saw killed," said Llalal, grimly. "The Noifs use criminals of their own people to experiment on, too. The time our men saw the weapon work, it was set to kill the Noifs and not harm Maureg or Walat . . ." He paused, staring at Jim. "And that," he said deliberately, "was what happened. I was there. I saw!"

"What'd you see?" demanded Jim.

"There were two of our people, two Walats and two Noifs," said Llalal. "All men condemned to death for crimes. They were made to stand in a tight group, touching, with the two Noifs in the center. The weapon was turned on, and the two Noifs fell. The others stood as they were, not understanding what had happened."

Jim found his jaw setting disbelievingly and forced it to relax. Maybe it's possible, he warned himself. Don't close the door on the chance. Keep an open mind. Besides, he added to himself, whether it's possible or not doesn't affect us.

"At any rate," said Jim, "I'm sorry. But I told

you we have business of our own that has to come
first with us—"

"Is it too much to ask that you go in with some
members of the Brotherhood to look at the weapon?"
said Llalal. "How can that be too much to ask? Our
people have crept in where the weapon is, in the big
storehouse cut half out of the inside of the mountain.
They have looked at it, but they do not understand it.
We have built another like it, but it does not work.
Soon the Noifs will have it perfected to work on a
huge scale and they will have the world for themselves!"

"No . . ." began Jim. But just then there was the
sound of feet and voices coming up the stairs, and a
second later, Curt and Ellen hurried into the room.
They stopped dead on seeing the two Mauregs.

"Llalal?" asked Curt, incredulously, looking at
the shipowner.

"The same," answered Llalal. "Your friend here
will explain." The desperation had gone out of him
suddenly. He smiled casually at them all. "We've
been chatting. Now, my friend and I have to go. A
good voyage to you all—to Annohne."

He turned to his companion.

"Come," he said, abruptly, and led the way out.
The three humans and Peep heard the Maureg footsteps going down the staircase outside their room.

"What's up?" began Curt in Quebahrian, turning
to Jim and Peep.

"We'd better talk in English," interrupted Jim. "Did you find a ship for us?"

"The *Kakkol,*" answered Ellen, "with a Walat skipper. It's a bigger ship than Llalal's was, with an actual hull and a hold. And he's got a crew of eight Walats. He said we could get over to Annohne in one day."

"Leave tomorrow morning, and get into Annohne by tomorrow evening," said Curt. "Say, what *was* Llalal doing here? How could he get here so quickly, anyway? We left him behind in Hekko Port, didn't we?"

Jim explained. He also repeated what Llalal and his companion had told them.

"So we're being watched, all right," Ellen said. "Won't that be dangerous when we get to Annohne and have to hunt for the beacon?" She looked at Peep.

"It *is* a potentially serious problem," said Peep, looking worried. He brightened suddenly. "But as you say, it is merely a matter of giving them the slip, which we can do by being less easily identified as a group. Now, suppose you went aboard this boat—the *Kakkol*—by yourselves, and then after you were aboard I quietly swam out—tsk!" said Peep, interrupting himself crossly.

"What's the matter?" asked Curt.

"I entirely forgot," said Peep, "on this low gravity world the impure hydrogen dioxide of which the ocean is constituted—as on your Earth, young friends—

is entirely too light for one of my mass to swim in. I would sink like a stone. In fact, like a nugget of gold, the relative weight of which my mass more nearly resembles. I have it!'' he cried happily, beaming at them.

"Pretend you're gold?'' asked Jim, skeptically.

"Why not?'' said Peep, excitedly. "Simply find a chest and a couple of stout Walats to carry me aboard the ship. To play safe I will even remain in the chest throughout the voyage.''

Jim argued. It was too elaborate a scheme, he thought. Also, he did not think that merely keeping Peep out of sight would throw their Maureg watchers off the trail. However, the other three were all in favor and when Ellen pointed out that he himself had said that he wanted to avoid a possible Walat challenge to combat, he finally agreed.

The next morning dawned dark and stormy. They located a cabinetmaker, bought an empty chest, and carried it to a conveniently deserted alleyway, where Peep climbed in. Then Curt went out, scouted up a couple of Walat porters, and with the porters carrying the chest, they proceeded down to the quay and on board the *Kakkol*.

They had just halted on board the *Kakkol*, when the two porters dropped the chest in relief and with a thump upon the deck planks of the ship.

"*Skevamp!*'' snapped the chest, on a note of irritation. The porters, who were standing facing them, stared at everyone and every place except at the chest.

"What was that?" asked one porter suspiciously. Jim had a sudden inspiration.

"Oh, just our pet bundii—in the box, here," he said.

The porters stared at him, and then broke into coughing laughter.

"Pet bundii!" sputtered one. "Pet pigs of iron! Break my head if I ever agree to carry a bundii that heavy again for such a small fee!"

The hint was obvious. Curt got busy paying off the porters.

As Ellen had said, the ship was larger than Llalal's. The passengers had been given a single large deck cabin, rather than the screen-partitioned areas they had aboard Llalal's ship. From the open window of that cabin—it was evidently the Quebahrian equivalent of a ship's lounge—they watched as the *Kakkol* was hand-towed by dock workers down to the end of the quay, and then floated away on the outgoing tide, while her sails filled, toward the sea.

Joffo was built on the inner curve of a sheltered bay. The bay waters themselves were only slightly choppy. But when they cleared the mouth of the bay and found themselves in open water, the boat began to roll violently. Soon Curt was extremely seasick, Ellen was anything but comfortable, and even Jim felt a little queasy.

Peep, however, when Jim lifted the chest lid in the

privacy of the cabin to check on the Atakit, proved to be completely unaffected by the motion of the ship. He lay comfortably on his back with his legs tucked up and his forearms crossed on his chest to fit into the small space inside the chest.

"Perhaps," he suggested to Jim, "we Atakits are not capable of becoming seasick. Come to think of it, I have never heard of the malady affecting one of my race. In any case, this is a golden opportunity for me to try and approach an actual trance state of meditation, as your Earthly mystics do in their Eastern lands. This too, to my knowledge, has never been accomplished by an Atakit before. But, who knows? At the moment I am concentrating on education, which like responsibility, is one of the wellsprings of nonviolence."

"Well, if you're all right," said Jim.

"I am eminently all right," replied Peep. "In fact, I am confidently expecting a revelation at any minute. So, if you will close the lid of the chest, young friend. . . . Call me, of course, if you need me for anything."

"Good luck," said Jim, and closed the lid. Seeing Ellen was in no mood to be sociable, and Curt had gone on deck, where he was leaning unhappily on the rail of the ship's side, Jim went out on deck to see if the air would help his queasiness. Eventually his stomach did settle down and even Curt recovered, so they returned to the cabin.

Ellen was standing over the chest.

"Jim," said Ellen, in English. "I can't seem to rouse Peep. Is he asleep, or what?"

Jim waited for the roll of the ship to help him, and then staggered to the center of the room where the chest was. Peep lay curled up as Jim had seen him last, his eyes closed. Jim reached down and prodded Peep's shoulder. It was like prodding fur stretched over solid rock.

"I've already poked him pretty hard," said Ellen, "but he doesn't stir. What's wrong with him?"

"He was trying to put himself in a trance," said Jim, unhappily. "Could be he made it. Of course, maybe he's just asleep, like you said. Come to think of it, has anyone ever seen him sleep before?"

The other two shook their heads.

"He was always awake whenever I looked at him or spoke to him," said Curt.

"Whatever it is," said Jim, scowling, "it's a fine time to have it happen. We should be getting briefed on Annohne."

There was nothing to be done about it. By late afternoon, the clouds had thickened until it was dark as twilight, and heavy seas were breaking over the deck of the ship, washing along her length and even swirling under the door to flood the carpets of the cabin. Suddenly, the door itself was torn open.

"Everybody out!" roared the Walat shipowner. "Everybody out and help throw cargo overboard. We're drifting on the reefs below Annohne harbor! I

need every pair of hands there are to lighten ship
before these seas break her part!''

A wave came sweeping down the deck and swirled
into the cabin, whirling around the Walat's knees and
half-submerging Peep's chest. Jim sloshed to the door
as the wave receded. Looking past the Walat's shoulder, he saw a distant line of darkness, cliffs under the
black sky, and white foam at their base. The white
foam was only a hundred yards or so away.

"You don't have time to lighten cargo," shouted
Jim. "Let's get your life raft off!"

"No!" cried the Walat. "I'm going to save my
ship." He drew his long sword. "Get outside and
start heaving cargo! Do you hear me? Get outside or
I'll kill you!"

"No!" shouted Jim. The Walat's sword swept up
with amazing swiftness. There was the twang of a
bowstring, sounding tinny and toylike in all the other
noise of the ship, and an arrow suddenly sprouted in
the shipowner's thick shoulder. Jim, glancing about,
saw Ellen, pale-faced, fitting another arrow to her
bow.

A hoarse cry from the doorway jerked his attention
back to the Walat who had dropped his sword to tug
at the arrow. Then a new wave swept him off his
feet, and he went down in a flurry of foam and was
carried off down the steeply slanting deck.

"Let's get to the raft!" shouted Jim, over his
shoulder to the others; but just then the ship seemed

to lift up and up, as if raised by a giant hand from the deeps below, and then flung forward.

There was a shock, a rending crash. Knocked off his feet, Jim saw the room, the chest, Ellen, Curt, and the very walls of the cabin itself tumbling in a wave of water around him. He flung out his arms, closed them on something solid, and clung.

Then the water thundered over his head, and it was the last thing he remembered.

11

"Jim!—*Jim!*"

It was Ellen's voice, calling him. It seemed to
come from a long way away in the darkness. For a
long moment Jim resisted hearing it. Wherever he
was, he was comfortable, and did not want to wake
up. But waking came in spite of what he wanted,
bringing with it a dull ache in his head, a sick feeling
in his stomach, and an overall feeling of icy coldness.

He lay on something flat and unyielding. He blinked
upward at the darkness and saw that it was real. He
blinked again and saw it was sky heavy with black
cloud, with only a few rusty-colored edges to show
the sunset hidden behind it. He moved his fingers
and closed them on a handful of hard-packed wet
sand. He turned his head and saw towering black

cliffs overhanging this little strip of beach littered with planks and timbers and dashed by furious surf.

Two faces moved between himself and the curtain of black cliff. They were the faces of Ellen and Curt.

"He's coming to," said Curt's voice.

"Wha . . . what's this?" Jim said thickly.

"Jim!" said Ellen, urgently. "Do you know us? Do you know who we are?"

"Sure . . . Ellen. Curt," muttered Jim. "What's the matter?" He tried to sit up and Curt helped him.

As he came to a sitting position, something like a heavy lead weight seemed to swing forward and strike him just behind the eyes. He groaned.

"My head!" he said, putting both hands up to it. His fingers came on a bump that felt as huge as a cantaloupe among the short hairs on the back of his skull. It was as tender as an open wound. Wincing, he took his fingers from it.

"You got hit by one of the cabin walls," said Ellen. "The whole cabin got washed off the ship and we hung on to it and rode the pieces ashore. Curt held on to you all the way. You were unconscious. If it wasn't for him . . ." She stopped.

Jim turned his head painfully to look at Curt.

"Thanks," he said.

"Well, you know—" said Curt, almost angrily, jerking his head aside to look away, out at the surf. "I just held on. That's all. You know!" He shrugged, still looking out to sea, then turned to face Ellen. "We've got to get someplace where we can warm up

and dry off.'' His teeth were chattering as he said it.
''That water wasn't too cold, but now, out here in
the wind . . .''

''Can you stand up, and walk, Jim?'' asked Ellen.

''Let me try,'' said Jim. With the other two helping, he stumbled to his feet, his head exploding with
pain at every jolt his body gave it. ''Yes, I'm all
right. Where to?''

''Let's go up along the foot of the cliffs,'' said
Curt. ''There must be a way to the top, or a cave, or
something—''

He broke off. A circle about ten feet in diameter
around them had suddenly been illuminated whitely.
Looking up, they saw the bright, glaring eye of what
could only be a powerful electric searchlight away up
on top of the cliffs, a hundred or more feet overhead.

''Stay where you are, O Mauregs!'' The thin,
almost musical voice of a Noif floated down to them.
''The Coast Watchers will reach you shortly!''

''The Coast Watchers!'' said Curt. ''I wonder
what—'' But Jim never heard the end of the sen-
tence. With the tilting back of his head to look up at
the searchlight the lead weights in his skull had gone
crashing backward. Pain flooded his head, and dizzi-
ness enveloped him in an abrupt, whirling cloak. He
felt himself falling and went spinning off into the
black depths of unconsciousness once more.

When he wakened again, he opened his eyes on a
lighted room with walls of either brick or brick-sized
stone that had been covered with a smooth gray

paint. He lay on something soft, he was warm and dry again, and his head did not ache. He heard the sound of voices and, turning his head, saw Curt and Ellen seated in chairs on the other side of the room, talking in low voices.

"Hi," said Jim to them, his own voice sounding strange in his ears, "where are we now?"

They looked up at the sound of his voice and came over to him. Meanwhile, he threw off the cape that had been covering him and sat up, swinging his legs over the side of what looked more like a padded table than a bed.

"How're you feeling?" Curt asked.

"Fine," said Jim. His fingers explored the back of his head and found it swollen and tender. But that didn't bother him as long as the headache was gone. He repeated, "Where are we?"

"We don't know," said Ellen.

"Don't know?" Jim stared at her.

"We're somewhere in the temple city of Annohne," said Curt. "We know that much. What we don't know is what this place is—a hospital, a hotel, or a jail."

"Jail!" repeated Jim. Curt nodded toward the door in the wall at right angles to the wall behind Jim's bed.

"The door's locked," said Curt, "and there are no windows. Notice?"

Jim looked around. There were, in fact, no windows. There was an archway opposite the closed door. Jim looked in that direction.

"There are a couple more rooms through there," said Curt, "but no way out of them. One of them's got running water like a bathroom. These Noifs are no slouches compared to the Mauregs and Walats. Notice the electric light?"

He pointed upward toward the ceiling of the room. Jim stared.

There was indeed an electric light in the ceiling, or something very like it. It was a glass container about the size and shape of a cigar box, with two black electrodes visible in it. The only strange thing about it was that it seemed to be filled with a semitransparent liquid, instead of vacuum or gas, as on Earth. The liquid glowed with a luminescence like the brilliant, greenish light emitted by "fire beetles," or southern click beetles, mistakenly called fireflies in certain areas of the Southern United States. Looked at directly, this greenish, powerful glow was hard on the eyes. Once, however, the light had bounced off the gray-painted walls it was not unpleasant.

"They brought in a Maureg and he put some kind of salve on your head," said Ellen. "I didn't know whether to stop him or not. We've been here overnight."

"Overnight!" said Jim. He broke off as the door Curt had said was locked suddenly opened. A small, grave-looking Noif stood in the doorway.

"O Friends," the Noif said pleasantly, "will you

come with me now?'' His pleasantness did not include any attempt to hide a weapon Llalal had called a spring-gun, which was slung over his shoulder.

''Where to?'' asked Jim, standing up.

''Our Temple Chief would like to talk to you—about your shipwreck, and other things. Will you come with me?''

There was nothing else to do. They followed him out of the room and down a gray-painted corridor and out into the watery sunshine of a day after a storm, the blue sky half obscured by torn masses of gray and white clouds mixed together in layers. A strong, cool wind whistled over the high walls of the courtyard and ruffled the short dun hair of the two aardarts harnessed to a closed coach with a boxlike body and a high seat in front where a Noif coachman sat.

Their Noif escort opened the door of the body of the coach and ushered them into it. Inside were two benches facing each other. Curt took the one facing backward, Jim and Ellen took the other facing forward. They heard their escort mount to the outside seat with the coachman, the noise of gates opening, and the coach began to move.

Jim tried the door of the coach quietly. It would not open. He leaned back in his seat and exchanged glances with Curt and Ellen.

''Seems, to me,'' he said, low-voiced and in English, ''that they must have had some way of hearing what went on in those rooms back there. That Noif came to the door almost as soon as I woke up.''

"Oh!" said Ellen, suddenly. He broke off and stared at her questioningly. "You haven't had anything to eat!" she said. "They fed us."

"Food," said Jim, grimly, "is the least of my worries. As a matter of fact, I don't feel very much like eating, anyway." He looked out the window for a second. The temple city of Annohne Island was a crowded but neat arrangement of buildings of mainly stone construction. Because most of the stone was dark, the whole town had a black look, like the color of the Noifs themselves. The result was a sober, businesslike atmosphere enhanced by the way the Noifs walked briskly, almost at a run, about the streets. Looking ahead, Jim saw a huge assemblage of towers and buildings that seemed half-carved out of the high black cliffs behind them.

"That must be the temple," said Jim, "it's where we're headed."

"That's right," said Ellen. "They pointed it out to us when they brought us up to the city from the beach where the Coast Watchers found us."

"Were any of the Walats found with us—" Jim broke off suddenly. "Peep!" he said. "What happened to Peep?"

Curt and Ellen looked at each other.

"We didn't see him, Jim," said Ellen, softly. "We never saw him after the cabin was washed off the ship."

"He probably never even woke up," said Curt. "I

know—we were hoping, too, Jim. But the Coast Watchers didn't find anybody but us.''

"Peep!" said Jim. "Drowned!" He could not believe it. He shook his head. It was inconceivable that someone as powerful as Peep could be finished without some large and furious battle. But, thought Jim bleakly, the ocean was not like a Walat, to be knocked out or tossed aside.

"We didn't want to believe it either," Ellen said sympathetically. "But you remember what Peep said about being far too heavy to swim. He must have gone down like a rock and taken that chest along with him."

Jim sat trying to absorb it all and not succeeding. Peep had always been something too good to be true, with his nonviolent philosophy, his uncontrollable temper, and his happy attitude toward the universe in general. But they had depended on him more than they had realized. They had depended on him, his strength, his knowledge—

"The beacon!" snapped Jim in English, turning on the other two. "Did Peep ever say where the beacon was here on Annohne?"

They looked back at him. Curt shook his head slowly.

"He never did say," said Curt, "and we never thought to ask him. Ellen and I thought of that almost as soon as they'd brought us here, and we knew you were going to come out of it all right."

Jim stared at them. He felt himself going colder and colder as he sat.

"Jim!" Ellen caught hold of his arm. "Jim! Are you all right?"

"Yes," he replied, shaking his head to free himself of the coldness. Slowly he pushed it away from him. Only a feeling of bitterness remained. Those who had been behind the breakdown of the spaceship had succeeded in their scheme. He had not been very clever after all, thought Jim, self-accusingly. He should at least have told Peep of his suspicions, even if it was unlikely that Peep would have believed his theory. If he had told Peep, and Peep had believed him, the little Atakit might still be alive.

And he, Curt, and Ellen would still have a chance to find the beacon and send for rescue.

He and the other two sat silent as the carriage wound through the streets and finally passed through a wide gate in which a full troop of armed Walats stood on guard, together with several Noifs armed with spring-guns. Their carriage rattled down several streets evidently within the grounds of the temple and pulled to a stop.

The carriage door was opened, and the Noif that had escorted them from their rooms, or one exactly like him, stood there.

"Come with me, O Friends," he said.

They followed. He led them up a flight of stone steps and into a maze of rooms and connecting corridors all made of gray-painted stone and illuminated

by the odd lights. For the first time, the humans saw
the Noif females and children. The interior of the
temple was alive with them and, if the males walked
fast, the women ran and the children charged. The
rooms rang with their high, musical voices.

"Peep did say they lived communally, in large
clans or families," said Ellen. Jim, looking sideways, saw her glancing around with almost professional interest. But before he had a chance to ask her
what else Peep had said about the Noif, their escort
opened a tall door and led them into a room where a
Noif sat alone behind a desk on which there were
papers, writing instruments like fine-tipped paint
brushes, and a spring-gun.

A small, bell-like instrument was also mounted on
one corner of the desk, and as they came up to stand
in front of the desk, this instrument sounded a series
of different-toned chimes.

The Noif behind the desk listened until the chiming stopped, and then reached out to the base of the
instrument. His fingers were busy there for a few
seconds, then he sat back and looked at Jim, Ellen,
and Curt.

"O Mauregs," he said, "you are strangers to
Annohne. Why did you come here to our island and
our city?"

"We're just traveling to see different places," Jim
said. "We heard about your island and it sounded
interesting. So we came here."

"Then you come from far away?" fluted the Noif.

"Yes," said Jim shortly.

The Noif looked away from them all and seemed to freeze in that position. With his body and trim head immobile, he suddenly looked to Jim like a large version of a chameleon, checking himself for no apparent reason to pose like a statue, the way those small lizards would do. Then the Noif moved again and looked back at them.

"Do you belong to the so-called Brotherhood among the Mauregs?" he asked.

"Brotherhood?" Jim asked. "I don't know what it is."

The Noif leaned forward, picked up the spring-gun lying on his desk and passed it across into Jim's hands.

"Have you ever handled one of these before?" he asked.

Jim looked at the weapon with curiosity, turning it over in his grasp so that he could examine the two projections from its center part, top and bottom. The top, he saw, was a frame loaded with small, tapering darts of metal not much bigger than a .30 caliber rifle bullet. These dropped into a firing chamber just ahead of small objects fed in from the magazine underneath the weapon. He examined the objects in this other magazine curiously. Evidently one of them popped up into place behind each dart in the magazine.

One of the lower objects came out in his hand. It seemed to be a flat coil of metal, like a small, thick spring squeezed into pancake shape. He turned it over curiously in his fingers.

"No," he said to the Noif. "Never."

"I believe you," said the Noif. He got up and reached across the desk to take the flat metal coil out of Jim's fingers and gingerly reinsert it in its magazine of the spring-gun. "You very nearly triggered the spring you were holding, and it would have torn off at least part of your hand if you had. But if not members of the Brotherhood, who are you?"

"I'll repeat," said Jim, a little grimly, "we're travelers. In fact we're castaways, and all we want to do is get out of here."

"Yes . . ." said the Noif. Once more he went motionless, and evidently lost in thought. Then he looked back again at the three of them.

"Time," he said, surprisingly, "is like the mechanism of the gun you were just holding. The compressed spring is triggered and expands, driving the dart before it. At the same time, the recoil of that expansion moves a new spring up and a new dart down into the magazine, ready to fire. It's just that way with this world of ours, today. We Noifs have a spring-gun in our heads, so to speak, and it solves each problem as we meet it, but each time it jacks up into position a new problem."

He looked from one to another of them, lined up in front of his desk.

"You have a bundii with you?" he asked.

"He drowned," said Ellen.

"I'm sorry. You must feel bad to lose such a pet. They are very affectionate we understand, and although we don't keep pets, we can imagine the attitudes of those who do," said the Noif. "Now, as I was saying about the spring-gun in our heads, we were all like bundii once—Noif, Maureg, and Walat. But the Noifs alone have set out to change things, because of the spring-gun in our heads. And we've changed them. In my own short lifetime, the world has been much changed by us."

He stared at them for a second.

"You understand?" he said. "After hundreds of thousands of years, suddenly we are beginning to change the world. And with each change we make, we make an enemy. The Walat feels we have taken away his chance for adventure and nobility, and the Maureg feels we are taking away his chance for happiness and his freedom. All because our tools are better tools than theirs, and still getting better these last two generations."

He stopped.

"Do you understand?" he said again.

"I follow you," said Jim. "We all follow you."

"We didn't set out to rule the Walat and the Maureg," said the Noif, "but by objecting to the natural use of the spring-gun in our hands, they force us into a conflict. And it is a conflict we must inevitably win." He looked at Jim. "If you have understanding, you must see that this is true. It's not

up to me or you; it's up to the spring-gun of time—
and it must happen.''

"All right," said Jim.

The Noif leaned forward over his desk.

"We know almost every step you've taken since
you appeared above the port of Chyk. Where you
were before that we have not yet traced, but we will
find out. Further we know—even if the Mauregs
themselves do not—that you are not like them. Even
your bundii is different. Can you deny this?''

"You're doing the talking," growled Jim.

"Then I ask you again," said the Noif. "Why did
you come here to our island and our city?"

He and Jim gazed at each other. The Noif's dark
eyes were like the eyes of the harbor master in
Chyk—like the eyes and the gaze of the physicists
Jim remembered in Research Three, back on Earth.

"I answered that," said Jim. "If you don't believe
me, I don't know what else to tell you."

The Noif sat back. He looked past the three of
them to their Noif escort.

"Take them," he told the escort. He looked back
at Jim. "If you have not decided to answer me
correctly by sunrise of tomorrow's day, we will con-
demn you as criminals, and use you as condemned
criminals are used. Think of it between now and
then.''

He looked back down at the papers on his desk.
The Noif escort came up alongside them.

"We will leave now," said the escort.

He took them out of the room and down a series of
corridors and then through a large room filled with
what looked like stamping machines. But what went
into the machines was a coil of metal about six
inches long and what came out, Jim saw as they
passed, were the flat little coils such as he had seen
in the spring-gun. For the first time he realized how
much energy must have been locked in the spring he
held, and as he remembered his handling of it, a faint
dampness sprang out on his forehead.

If the metal of which the coils were made was
anything like good Earthside spring steel, he could
indeed have lost part of his hand, had the spring
suddenly gone into its expanded position. Incredulity
stirred in him. Llalal had said that the seemingly
primitive Mauregs had successfully duplicated *this?*
Jim stared at the fifteen-foot-tall compressing machines in disbelief.

But they were being taken on, down another series
of corridors. Jim figured that by now they must be
well back in the mountain behind the temple. They
stopped before a door, which their escort opened. He
ushered them in, and closed the door behind them.
Jim heard a bolt snick to on the outside of the door.

Just to make sure, he tested the door and found it
would not open. It was a room identical with the one
they had been in before the escort had come to get
them. And off it was another room, from which came
the faint, steady sound of running water.

The same light in the ceiling illuminated carpets

and some padded tufts like cushions, thick enough to make low seats. Ellen sank down onto one of these. Curt went into the other room and came out again.

"Just like the other place," he said. He looked at the light in the ceiling. "I suppose that's the same and never goes out, either." He, too, sat down on one of the tufts and Jim followed his example.

"Maybe we should have made a break for it while we were in the carriage," said Curt, as if he was thinking aloud.

"Not much use," said Jim. "The local populace seems to be ninety percent Noifs, and they'd probably have helped catch us."

"How'd we get into this mess?" said Curt, but without any fire in the words. "If you'd told me about this back on Earth, I just wouldn't have been able to swallow it."

Jim opened his mouth. He was about to tell them about his suspicions that some group in the Federation wanted the human students to get into trouble, if not to disappear completely.

And how events had now proved him right. But he stopped himself just in time.

It could do no good to tell Curt and Ellen this now, and it would just make them feel worse. If they all had only a handful of hours before they were used as experimental subjects for the Noifs' selective weapon, or whatever it was Llalal and the other Mauregs had seen, it was little enough for Jim to do to keep his knowledge to himself.

"Look," he said, trying to sound cheerful. "I've evidently been sleeping for hours and I'm wide awake. But why don't you two try to get some sleep. Maybe after you get some rest we can think of something—"

He broke off. An uncarpeted section of the floor before his tuft had suddenly cracked with a dull noise and heaved upward, revealing the ends of some bricks. Dirt and broken stone spilled out around the break, which now showed itself like a black and ragged hole about six inches in diameter. From this came a momentary scuffling sound as of rubble being kicked aside and then a sharp and dusty nose with dusty whiskers stuck up through the hole into the room.

"Forgive me, young friends," said the nose, "for being so long in rejoining you. But the situation has been somewhat complicated."

12

"Peep!" screamed Ellen.

Jim and Curt were staring at the hole. There was another upward explosion of bricks. Peep climbed up onto the floor before them and stood covered with white stone powder and dust.

He sneezed. It was a small, neat sneeze like the sneeze of a cat.

"Ah, young friends," he said, having sneezed.

"We thought you were drowned!" said Curt.

"Did you?" said Peep, suddenly unhappy. "Dear me. Dear me! Of course. Naturally! How could you think anything else?" He dealt himself a sledge-hammer blow on the temple. "Later, I suspected you might have thought so. But no. Actually," said Peep, looking guilty, "in the process of achieving a

199

trance state of concentration, I seem to have dozed off.''

He looked remorsefully at them.

"I suppose you may have known this. You tried to wake me?"

"Yes," said Jim.

"I should have told you earlier," said Peep, unhappily, "that we Atakits, while we need relatively little sleep, are what you might characterize as heavy slumberers, once we drop off." He sighed. "I woke up, as it happened, on my own. But by that time I was on the bottom of the ocean. Fairly shallow ocean, of course. I seemed to be on the seaward side of some reefs."

Jim and Curt stared at him.

"But," said Curt. "Didn't you—I mean, why didn't you drown?" He fumbled for a second. "You told us you were too massive to swim in the sea water, here."

"Quite true," Peep replied, "absolutely true, of course. But I omitted to mention the additional and inevitable corollaries of that inability. While I could not swim, I could with very little difficulty walk along the bottom until I came to shore—even in what I believe you, young friends, would consider fairly heavy seas and surf. It took me some little while to reach the beach, of course, which was why you were gone when I arrived. But I was never in any real danger." There was the sound of rushing footsteps and of a door closing behind Jim, but both he and Curt were too fascinated to look around.

"But . . . but you breathe *air!*" said Curt. "How could you walk ashore underwater without breathing?"

"Correction, young friend." Peep held up a professorial hand. "Like you, I breathe atmosphere. But, also like you, I am sustained by *oxygen*. And there is oxygen in the sea water both here and back on your Earth, just as there is in the air."

They stared at him.

"But," began Jim, scowling, "are you telling us you breathed water . . . ?"

"Indeed," Peep said earnestly. "Why not? You may not be aware of it, but as far back as the early 1960's on your own Earth some human scientists were proving it was possible for mice, and even dogs, to breathe water and absorb the necessary oxygen from it into their lungs. True, the animals required selective anesthesia to overcome instinctive reflexes that closed their windpipes against the entrance of any fluid. And the water had to be unusually heavily saturated with oxygen. But it was done."

"But look here," said Jim, "the sea water here can't be extra-saturated with oxygen. I mean, I haven't tested it or anything like that, so I don't actually know. But it stands to reason—"

"Oh, it is not," said Peep, quickly. "However, you overlook one small item. I am, because of my birth on a heavy gravity world, somewhat more powerful physically than yourselves. While your lungs—

and I am sure that they are superb lungs, young friends—'' interjected Peep anxiously, ''might have some slight difficulty in pumping anything as heavy as water in and out at a high rate of speed, it is hardly any trouble at all for my own chest muscles to do so. By, you might say, *panting* slightly, I can breathe impure hydrogen dioxide almost as successfully as the atmosphere of this world. Or yours.''

''But then what—'' began Curt, and broke off in midsentence. He looked around. ''Where's Ellen?'' he asked Jim. ''I thought she was sitting right behind us.'' He spotted the closed door to the other room. ''You think something's wrong?'' he said, suddenly alarmed, getting up from his tuft and striding over to the door.

''Ellen!'' he called.

There was no answer.

Curt went a little pale. ''You don't suppose one of the Noifs sneaked in when we were talking?'' He rapped on the door. *''Ellen!''*

''Go away!'' responded Ellen's rather cross and muffled voice.

''There's something wrong,'' Curt said. ''She never sounded like that before. Maybe we better break down the door.''

Jim shook his head. The sound of Ellen's voice had reassured him.

''You don't have any sisters?'' he asked Curt.

''No,'' said Curt, puzzled. ''Why?''

"Women," explained Jim, raising his eyebrows at the closed door.

"Oh," said Curt.

"Better leave her alone," said Jim. "She'll come out after a while. She's been real good about things all the time so far."

"That's right, she has," said Curt, coming back and sitting down. "Go on, Peep. You got ashore, and—" he broke off. "Say, we ought to be getting out of here before the Noifs come along and find us with Peep here and a hole in the floor."

"I don't think there's any real need for haste," said Peep. "This area is generally deserted by the Noifs of the Temple Family between sunset and sunrise the following morning. Besides, they will be at one of their Gatherings, now."

"Gatherings?" asked Jim.

"Why yes, a Noif family social function. The Noifs are emotionally very close to each other—but I told you that."

"No," said Jim.

"Didn't I? That's right, it was our young friend in the other room. She had a marvelously inquiring mind. At any rate, we're safe for the moment," said Peep, "and there are things I must discuss with you before we leave."

"Just a minute," said Jim. "Before you say another word, where's the rescue beacon?"

"As a matter of fact, that bears on what I was about to say," said Peep embarrassedly. "It is in this temple, in a room which also holds the Noif selective weapon of which Llalal spoke to you."

"It is? What's that got to do with it?" asked Curt.

"I will start at the beginning," said Peep.

"Go ahead," said Jim, scowling at Curt. "We'll listen until you're through."

"I emerged on the beach," said Peep. "As you know, it was night. However, the glow of lights from the city here could be seen above the cliffs in one direction, and I believed you would probably have gone in that direction provided you, young friends, had also gotten to shore safely."

"That's right," said Jim. "You couldn't know if we were safe, either."

"Luckily, however," continued Peep, "I soon came across a sort of road leading up to the top of the cliff and—the moon happening to come out at that moment—I saw a number of recent footsteps in the sand headed up it. Some of the footsteps were Noif, but the others were unmistakably human. You may not have noticed it, young friends, but you have a definite tendency to walk on your heels rather than on your toes as the Mauregs do."

"I didn't know that—go on," said Jim hurriedly, seeing Curt was scowling at him for his interruption.

"I made it to the top of the cliff and eventually into the city," said Peep. "I realized then that I could not locate you without some help. Accordingly, I went down to the waterfront, to the Maureg section, and went around to Mauregs, saying 'Llalal?

Llalal?' in limited, bundii fashion. And after several hours a Maureg came looking for me and said soothingly that he would take me to Llalal."

"Did he?" asked Curt, leaning eagerly forward on his tuft.

"He did," said Peep. "It turned out that Llalal and his friend had, in defiance of local sailing habits, set sail for here the night before we left—in fact, the moment they left us at the inn. Accordingly, they missed the storm and came safely to Annohne before us. This strange Maureg, one of their Brotherhood, it seems, took me to Llalal, who asked me about you."

"Did you talk to him? Intelligently, not bundii-style, I mean?" asked Jim.

"I took a venture," said Peep. "I knew he already was of the opinion that I was something more than an ordinary bundii, just as you three were something more than ordinary Mauregs. So I talked quite freely to him—not as I am speaking to you now, but in considerably more than the vocabulary an ordinary bundii could possess, although I used my words in a simple and primitive style. I told him that I thought you were in the hands of the local Noifs, and he had me wait for several hours while his agents of the Maureg Brotherhood checked around. At the end of that time they announced that I was correct. By this time, it was almost morning, and we began to lay plans to rescue you."

"But you didn't," said Curt.

"Before our plans could be put into execution,"

Peep continued, "the Noifs transferred you to the temple itself. At which point rescue became a great deal more difficult and risky. You could be rescued, but to do so, the Mauregs would have to risk having the Noifs find out that Mauregs had ways in and out of the Noif temple via the ventilating system. Once this fact was known, the Noifs would undoubtedly block off this way of ingress. So valuable do the Brotherhood consider the route, that they have permitted some of their own people to die as Noif prisoners, rather than give away the existence of such a route by rescuing them."

"Go on," said Jim, grimly, as Peep paused.

"Now," said Peep, "I was demanding that they risk this route in order to rescue you, young friends. I told them that if they would only show me how to reach your place of confinement I would be able to effect your rescue without help from them. But they hesitated, even at that. Finally, I was forced to bargain with them."

There was the sound of an opening door behind Jim and Curt, and footsteps. Ellen had come back into the room.

"I was forced to promise," said Peep, seriously, "that in return for their showing me how to get to you, you would do as Llalal has asked you, and see if you can help them with understanding and duplicating the Noifs' selective weapon."

"You did!" said Jim. "Did you have to agree to that?"

"I'm afraid so," confessed Peep. "As I mentioned earlier, the rescue beacon we must activate to be picked up from Quebahr is in the room with the weapon. This room was only a storeroom evidently, at the time the beacon was set up. But the room is now top secret, and closely guarded. Only by the ventilator route and with the help of the Brotherhood, can we hope to reach it."

He stopped and looked at them all seriously.

"When I take you with me now," he said, "it will be into the ventilators running above the tier of rooms underneath us. We will have to follow those ventilators back to the main shaft, and there, Llalal and his friends will be waiting for us, to take us directly to the room of the weapon. There's no way we can avoid keeping the bargain I made."

Jim looked at him for a second, then stood up and grinned.

"That's all right!" he said. "It's a lot better than what we were facing before you came through the floor. But we better get out of here."

"Ellen," said Curt. "Are you all right?"

"Of course I'm all right!" said Ellen. "Don't I look all right?"

"You do," said Curt. "But," he looked embarrassed, "I thought I heard you crying in there—"

"Certainly not!" snapped Ellen. "I just went in to wash my face. It's none of your business, anyway, what I do." She ran to Peep and threw her arms around him. "Oh, Peep!" she said, hugging him. "Why didn't you tell us you couldn't drown?"

"I fear I didn't think of it," he said apologetically.

"Come on, come on!" said Jim. "Let's get out of here. How do we go, Peep?"

"I will have to make the opening in the floor larger," said Peep. He bent down and ripped up several more square feet of floor. "Will that do?"

"It's ample," said Jim. "But what about the Noifs when they come in the morning? Won't it be plain we've gone into the ventilating system?"

"I plan," said Peep, "to tear another hole in the roof of the room beneath us, which is unlocked. Then, when we go, I will pile up rubble to block the way by which we escape, as if it was blocked by the falling of blocks from above." He began to lower himself into the hole. "I shall go first," he said, "to catch you as you jump down."

He disappeared into the blackness below. They followed him down. They found themselves in a tunnel about seven feet high but only about three feet wide, like a piece of rectangular ductwork from a heating system back home set on its side. They squeezed past Peep and waited while he tore a hole in the floor of the ductwork, then backed off and heaped rubble behind them. When the tunnel was effectively blocked, he squeezed past them once more to take the lead.

"We had better hold hands, young friends," he said.

Sidling along in the darkness, hanging on with his left hand to Peep's small paw, that felt like leather-covered steel, and with his right hand to Ellen's equally small, but softer fingers, Jim found himself thinking. He thought rather smugly that for once it was Curt who had said the wrong thing to Ellen, instead of himself. Not that it made any difference, of course. Mentally he began to calculate what percentage of wrong things said to Ellen he would say compared to Curt. The results were not encouraging. Counting back as well as his memory would let him, Jim figured that for every ten things he himself was likely to say that would rub Ellen the wrong way, Curt was only likely to say about one and a half.

At last they began to see the glow of light ahead and it grew stronger as they approached, until they could see each other clearly. A few seconds later they stepped through into what was obviously the main shaft, ten feet wide from wall to wall, and filled with at least a couple of dozen Mauregs waiting around a burning lantern set on the floor.

Peep let go of Jim's hand and Llalal emerged from the crowd to grip it.

"Brother!" he said. "You're with us!"

"I'll do what the bundii promised I would," said Jim, looking the Maureg steadily in the eye. "I'll try to help you with this weapon of the Noifs. But I don't guarantee anything. It may be just as baffling to me as it is to you."

"That you try," said Llalal, "is all we ask." He

wrung Jim's hand and let it go. "We've men already up in all the ventilation shafts leading into the room. When we get there, we'll take care of the guard and then hold the room as long as you need to work with the weapon . . ." He hesitated. "How long will you need, do you think?"

"How can I tell until I see it?" Jim asked. He scowled, affected by the deep emotion in Llalal's voice and manner, which he had not expected. "Don't you know the chances are that I won't understand it? The long odds are that I won't be able to do anything for you."

"We are the Brotherhood of long odds," said Llalal. "That a people may survive will a man not try anything?"

He looked keenly at Jim, then turned away and began giving orders. With the three humans and Peep in their midst, and a Maureg in the lead carrying the lantern, the group flowed through the main shaft. For the first time, looking around him, Jim saw that the Mauregs were armed with spring-guns—either those made by the Noifs or such exact duplicates that it was impossible to tell the difference.

Llalal walked beside Jim. Jim turned to him.

"These are spring-guns you made yourselves?" he asked. Llalal nodded, his green eyes bright on Jim's face.

"You mean you've built machines that can compress the springs the guns are loaded with, too?"

"Of course, Brother," said Llalal. His face lit for

a moment with pride. "That is where the Noifs make their mistake. We have always been clever with our minds as well as our hands. Have we not made pottery and glass and clocks and tools from the beginning, while the Walats fought and the Noifs argued and pondered? We can duplicate anything the Noifs can build, once we have seen it. Only—only we duplicate this weapon of theirs, and it doesn't work."

Jim was sorely puzzled. The ability to duplicate the compressing machines implied technical abilities of a high order. How could such abilities draw a blank with this weapon—whatever it was?

For that matter, all of Quebahr was puzzling. When they had first come down the volcano's side to Chyk, he had figured that the three races on Quebahr had reached about the equivalent of fifteenth- or sixteenth-century Europe as far as their technical civilization went.

But in some ways, they were much more advanced. And they seemed to be in the middle of a sort of technical revolution, which didn't go with primitive sailing vessels and nomadic tribes, and so forth. Quebahr was a sort of crazy quilt of ancient and modern seen from a human's point of view. Of course, thought Jim, he was looking at it from the outside, and—he felt a sudden sense of shock—what made him think every world had to follow exactly the path of technical and scientific development that Earth had taken?

He was still trying to absorb this new and startling thought when the group around him halted suddenly. Jim saw that they were standing just back of a large wire grille set in the wall. Beyond the wire grille was a brightly lighted room almost as big as the converted warehouse back on Earth that had housed Research Three.

Now, as Jim watched, one Maureg put his spring-gun to his shoulder and stepped up to the side of the grille. He sighted. There was a sudden muffled *spung* from his spring-gun. He lowered it and peered out through the grille.

"Perfect!" he said. "And the men at the other grilles got the other guards at the same time. All of them. We can break out these grilles now, and get inside."

Five minutes later Jim was standing almost beside the weapon. It was impossible to mistake it. It was mounted on large wheels as high as Jim's head and about twenty feet apart. The weapon itself appeared to be a mass of boxes and cables and smaller wires mounted upon a ten-foot-high carriage and reached by a sort of ladder.

Jim climbed the ladder and a curious prickling sensation passed over the back of his neck as he looked at what were evidently gauges and a sort of vernier control calibrated in figures he could not read. From his high perch, he looked around the room. Directly in front of the weapon was a tank like the tank at Research Three, and an adjoining and connected series of tanks filled with fish and water animals. Jim spotted a large fish like the one that had followed Llalal's boat and eaten the food Curt had thrown overboard.

Searching around, he found a hand crank that controlled the direction in which the most distant box of the assortment that together made up the shape of the weapon, was pointing. He cranked it around until it pointed at the big fish.

Nothing happened. He looked at the vernier again, and saw it was resting at one end of the scale. He moved the vernier carefully down the scale. Suddenly, the fish thrashed in its tank and went still, drifting like a dead thing.

Cautiously, without touching anything else, Jim climbed down from the weapon. Llalal met him at the foot of the ladder.

"Brother?" said Llalal. "You understand it?"

"I don't know," said Jim, unhappily. He looked at the distant fish, now floating on the surface of the water in its tank. "You said you made a weapon just like this?"

Llalal nodded.

"And you tried it on a fish like that?"

"Among other subjects," said Llalal, "yes."

"But you didn't set that little pointer and scale—"

"Indeed," said Llalal. "From the ventilating grille we observed with ship's telescopes every move made by the Noifs in using it, and the one time we were able to get in here when guards were absent, we used this original weapon, and it worked for us. It killed."

"It killed?" asked Jim. "The subjects didn't become conscious after, say, an hour or so?"

"What are you saying?" asked Llalal. "We could not wait around for an hour afterward—but why and how could they come back to life?"

"I don't know," Jim scowled. He walked around the base of the weapon, looking at it. He saw Curt and Ellen watching him, but not Peep. He came all way around to the other side and saw two ropelike objects that were pretty evidently insulated cables running to the machine. He kicked them, and a sudden stomach-chilling suspicion came to him.

"These—" he found there was no Quebahrian word for them, "these pipes-like-ropes. You duplicated them exactly, too?"

Llalal's slightly golden features tensed with what was obviously a strong effort to understand Jim's words.

"But why?" he said, at last. "We are not like the Noifs who cannot see in the dark."

"What's seeing in the dark got to do with it?" Jim asked.

"Why, we do not need the light up there!" Llalal pointed to one of the Noif liquid electric lamps that was built in at the top of the weapon. "We would rather have it, as we enjoyed the use of the lantern in the ventilating system, just now. But we did not have to have light to use the weapon, as the Noifs did, and it would have been foolish to go to the great work of building a light-pumping machine, such as the Noifs must have to make light and pump it into a lamp like that or these others.'' And he pointed to the lights burning high up in the ceiling of the room.

"Is that what you think goes through these?" Again Jim kicked the cables at his feet.

"Brother, what else?" asked Llalal, staring at him. "Any fool can see that these lamps of the Noifs are dark and empty of light until their light-pumping machine is turned on. Then the light is made in the machine and pumped through these ropes to the lamp.'' He suddenly clutched Jim's arm. "What is it? Does the weapon require light to work? We can move ours out into sunlight. Or if need be we can even build the light-pumping machines, themselves, if there is some particular virtue or usefulness in their light. Tell us, Brother!''

Jim shook his head.

"I don't know yet," he said, "I'm just asking questions. Let me talk to my friends for a moment privately.''

"Very well.'' Llalal fell back, beckoning the other Mauregs who were close to move back with him. Jim beckoned his companions over into the shadow of the weapon.

"Listen,'' he said, low-voiced and in English when they were close.

"There's something I've got to talk over with you.

But first—hadn't we better see if we can't find the beacon?''

"I have found it already, young friend," answered Peep in the same language. "And I have set it off. Rescue should arrive soon."

"Not soon enough to help us now," said Jim, grimly. He turned to Curt and Ellen. "You two have got to help me," he went on. "You've got to help me make up my mind about something. I don't include Peep because he's not human and it's my human knowledge that makes this decision necessary. Do you follow me?"

"No," said Curt.

"I mean," said Jim, slowly, "you two and I have got to decide whether I tell the Quebahrians something. I don't mean just the Mauregs, but the Noifs and the Walats as well. If I tell them and they understand me—and there's no reason they shouldn't be able to understand from what I've seen in this room—then this world will never be the same again."

"But—" began Ellen. She did not have time to finish.

Interrupting her, across the silence of the big room, came the sudden rattling of a latch from the double doors that gave entrance to it. Then the doors creaked as if weight was being put against them. But their lock evidently held. The creaking ceased.

"O Mauregs!" cried a high, musical Noif voice from beyond the doors. "We know you are in there. Also we know that you could only have entered by the ventilating system. Armed men of our race are now searching the system to find their way to you. Shortly you will be trapped between them and us. Surrender now and you will be well treated until the hour of your death.''

The voice fell silent. The whole huge room was silent. Human and Maureg, they stood looking at each other, without a word.

13

Llalal came swiftly across the floor to Jim. His face was fierce with pride.

"We do not surrender to Noifs," he said, "but, Brother, you and your friends must leave soon, if we are to get back through the ventilating system before they find all the escape routes and block them on us. In the fourth part of the period measured by an hourglass, it will be too late and we all must die here. This is nothing for us of the Brotherhood, but you are the hope of our people with your knowledge that may understand the weapon."

"You go," said Jim. "We'll wait here."

"No," said Llalal. "We would never go and leave you behind. Not even if you demanded it." He stared into Jim's eyes. "You have a few minutes more to decide for all in this room."

"All right," said Jim grimly, as Llalal turned and left. These last words of Llalal's combined with what he had discovered about the Noifs' weapon, had finally brought Jim to the point of decision. But there was one question to ask first. He turned to Peep.

"You say you set off the beacon?" he asked in English. "Did it work all right?"

"I assume so, young friend," answered Peep, looking inquiringly at him. "These beacons are not designed to fail."

I'll bet they aren't, thought Jim to himself. But are they designed not to be sabotaged? Whatever anti-Earth group among the Federation Aliens had wrecked the spaceship and gotten them all cast away here on Quebahr would not have forgotten a simple matter like fixing the rescue beacon so it would not work. In his own mind, Jim was convinced that the beacon had failed. That meant he and the others were stuck here unless the attention of the Federation could be attracted to Quebahr by some other means. And sight of the Noif weapon, thought Jim, had just suggested that means. But he would need the agreement of Ellen, Curt, and Peep.

"Listen," he said, turning to Curt and Ellen, "do you realize what this so-called weapon of the Noifs really is?"

They both shook their heads.

"Well, it isn't exactly the same device as I was

working around, on my part-time job where they were doing time-gap research for the faster-than-light drive back on Earth,'' said Jim. ''But it—this weapon—must use the same principle. The only thing is, it's no good as a weapon. That's why the Noifs are still having trouble with it.''

''What do you mean?'' asked Curt.

''I mean it's no good as a weapon for the Noifs,'' answered Jim. ''I didn't pay much attention to what Llalal's friend was saying about it at the Joffo inn until he said that at the weapon's present stage of development it could kill Noifs without hurting Mauregs or Walats. The Noifs, he said, hoped to work it around into a weapon that would kill Mauregs and Walats but not hurt Noifs. Now,'' said Jim, scowling, ''maybe it's possible to make a weapon that's selective—one that will kill one race and not harm another at all. But it's hard for me to believe it, when you're dealing with three races on one world that all eat the same food, drink the same water, breathe the same air and so forth.''

''But,'' said Ellen, ''Llalal said he *saw* Noifs killed and the Mauregs and Walats not touched.''

''That's just it,'' said Jim. ''That's what started me thinking. In our time-gap research, the sharks got hit hardest by no-time gaps, then the other selachians like the rays, then fish of all kinds, then the amphibians, getting less and less affected as you worked toward the warm-blooded creatures like humans. That's why I tried the weapon on that large fish in the tank there—'' Jim pointed at the fish still floating belly up. "It was knocked cold. Now Peep said that the ancestors of the Noifs were cold-blooded more recently than the ancestors of either the Mauregs or Walats; and that's probably the reason this device hits them so hard and doesn't so much affect the Walats and Mauregs.''

"But why don't the Noifs see this?'' Curt began.

"Because," answered Jim, "the Noifs are thinking of it *only* in terms of a weapon, instead of anything else—such as an element in a faster-than-light drive, for example.''

"Hold on!'' Curt interrupted excitedly. "You aren't saying that these Noifs have part of a space drive? You can't mean that! How can they have something like that without knowing the Theory of Relativity? And you don't mean to stand there and tell me they know Einstein's work—on a planet like this?''

"No," said Jim, "naturally not. But that's the joker. I felt just like you until I saw this room, here. I just naturally assumed that you couldn't do the kind of research I saw at the place where I worked, without all the modern knowledge we've got back home. But then it suddenly hit me—you don't have to know the Einsteinian Theories to make a time-gap transmitter!''

The other two humans stared at him.

"I don't understand," said Ellen, after a long second.

"Look," said Jim, urgently. "There's the Heisenberg Uncertainty Principle—do either of you know it? I can't explain it now, but the point is, the Noifs could arrive at this principle without knowing any-thing about the universe as we know it—I mean without knowing anything about the idea of travel to other planets of other stars. Then to get from that to time-gap research, all they would have to have would be some idea of radiation and the process of genera-tion of radio waves."

"You mean that, just that, would give them this, what did you call it? This time-gap business?" asked Curt.

"No, of course not," said Jim. "But it would bring them close enough so that in blind experiment-ing they could stumble on it, the way things are so often stumbled on in pure research. The point is, it's happened. Here's the device, over our heads right now. And what am I suppose to do about it?

"I can turn this world upside down and inside out!" said Jim. "Here's the situation. These three races have all got different slants—talents, I suppose you'd call them. The Noifs are natural pure re-searchers, theoreticians . . ." He pointed at the weapon. "This thing proves it. And the Mauregs are excellent technicians. Llalal tells me they can copy anything the Noifs make and have it come out as good or better. On the other hand, they've got no grasp of theory. You know why their copy of this weapon didn't work?"

"No," said Ellen, sounding interested. "Why?"

"Because they didn't include a power source!" Jim stared at them. "Can you beat it? They thought of the electric cables in terms of hollow ropes that channel a flow of light to the light fixtures. How do you like that? They could grasp the spring principle of the spring-guns because that's mechanical, but the nonmechanical theory of electrical current just doesn't exist for them until someone explains it to them. But do you see what a team they and the Noifs would make?''

He waited. Slowly, Curt and then Ellen nodded also.

''Now,'' Jim went on, ''add in the Walats. They're the adventurers, the risk-takers. The ones to put to use the devices and tools the Noifs dream up and the Mauregs build. Talk about a space-going combination. The Noifs could dream up the spaceships, the Mauregs could build them, and the Walats could crew them. Those Walats would jump at the chance.''

Curt and Ellen were gazing at him, open-eyed. Surprisingly, though, they didn't seem to be catching fire from his enthusiasm.

''Well,'' he said, ''I can make this happen. I'm telling you two about this rather than Peep, because—'' He broke off. ''Where's Peep?''

But Peep had disappeared again.

''Well, never mind,'' said Jim. ''Time's short. The point is, I can start this for them, just by speaking up. All I have to do is clear up Llalal's mistake about electric current and explain what can be done with it as a power source. And one more thing. Point out to them that the idea came originally from the Noifs and

the Noifs can be the source of more ideas if the
Mauregs will only work with them, instead of against
them.''

''But,'' said Ellen, ''why should the Noifs want to
work with the Mauregs? You said the Noifs had the
ideas.''

''Have you ever had anything to do with someone
who's got a good technical slant?'' asked Jim, turning to her. ''In ten minutes he can think up more and
better ways of putting a good idea to use than you'd
have thought possible in ten years. If I explain electricity to Llalal and his Mauregs, in six months they'll
be ahead of the Noifs in its application and use. The
Noifs'll have to come to them.''

He paused and looked at Curt.

''And once they start working together, the Walats
have to be drawn into it,'' he said. ''In ten years this
world could step forward into the equivalent of the
beginning of our twentieth century back on Earth. In
twenty years' time they could be coming up with a
space drive and be qualifying for Federation membership. And, of course, the Federation's attention
would be attracted to this world long before that—
probably in a year or two from now, once the Noifs
start broadcasting radio signals into space.''

He paused again to see if they were understanding
him.

''I see,'' said Curt, slowly, ''you think maybe you
shouldn't tell the Mauregs about electricity, then?''

Jim stared. He blinked at Curt. That had not been at all what he had been thinking.

"Well, I think you're right to be worried about it," Curt went on, evidently misunderstanding completely Jim's look. The tall young man's own face was drawn and serious. "Look, I know you don't think as much of history as you do, say, of physics . . ."

"Go on," said Jim, wonderingly.

"Well, it's just that history has its laws too. Cause and effect. One thing leads to another," said Curt. "Now that holds as true here as it does back on Earth. The steam engine brought on the industrial revolution and created the whole situation out of which the nineteenth and even the twentieth century grew. I mean that the steam engine ended up creating situations we were stuck with, as late as when you and I and Ellen were born."

He stopped.

"All right," said Jim. "I can see that. But the situations that can come out of this can't be anything but good. Wasn't a technical situation good for us on Earth? Didn't it bring us to the point where now we're going to join the Federation just as soon as we can get a faster-than-light drive going?"

"Sure, but can you be certain it's going to be just as good here where things are different?" asked Curt. "Look, I know I was an Archaist back on Earth, and that's a crazy sort of thing to be. But I was looking at history then from the inside. You can see it from the outside, the way it is here, and it makes you think. Anyway, I tell you—if I were back on Earth right now, I wouldn't be an Archaist any longer. And I'd be a lot less sure of how certainly any one cure I or anybody else came up with would make the future a rosy place to live in."

"But you aren't giving me a definite reason not to tell them!" said Jim. "You're just saying, 'Look out; this may turn out to have some bad effects. I can't guess what they might be, but maybe there'll be some.' But I tell you scientific knowledge and technology turned out nothing but good in the long run for people on Earth. Just give me one reason why it should be different here?"

"I'll give you one!" said Ellen, heatedly. "It could be different here because this is Quebahr, not Earth."

Jim looked down at her.

"But it's just the same—" he began exasperatedly.

"It is *not* the same!" snapped Ellen. "Curt saw some of the differences, because he's interested in history, and history has to do with people. But you didn't see any because your interests are all in science, and on an Earthlike world like this one, the basic physical and chemical laws are pretty much the same. So you took it for granted the people on Quebahr were the same, too. Well, they aren't!"

"In what way?" asked Jim.

"In culture, in history, in attitude—in everything!" Ellen replied. "Our forward steps in science and technology on Earth came about under the pressure of almost continuous wars down through known history. Quebahr's had nothing like that. We think automatically in terms of continental masses and the great populations that are in contact, on such large chunks of land. But Quebahr is a mass of islands that never permitted large states and countries to form. Let alone the fact that this world has three intelligent races sharing it, instead of one! That alone is enough of a difference from us so that no human can say he is sure *how* Quebahrians will react to a sudden, great scientific step forward like the one you're talking about!''

She stopped, and took a deep breath.

''All right,'' said Jim, scowling, ''suppose you're both right. You still haven't given me one good reason why these people, whatever they are, shouldn't be helped forward into the future. They can't stand still. Heck, they aren't standing still now! They've got to move forward, they're going to move forward anyway, why not help them? Well?''

He glared at Curt and Ellen and suddenly noticed that Peep was back.

''Peep,'' he said, ''what about it? Aren't I right? Why shouldn't I say the word to Llalal that'll save them years of fighting and experimenting and struggle? Aside from everything else, once I tell Llalal, he and his men will have to escape to get the knowledge back to their people. That's saving lives right there. What do you think? Tell me?''

"I cannot tell you, young friend," said Peep, twitching his whiskers sympathetically. "I am not the one faced with the problem, you see, and so I cannot know all the unconscious as well as the conscious factors involved in your consideration of it. But I would point out two things. One, the time in which Llalal and his men can escape is now growing very short. Two, if you did not feel unsure about giving the Mauregs this information, why did you ask others for their possible objections in the first place?"

"Why," said Jim. "I wasn't asking for possible objections—"

He broke off. Abruptly, the words died in his throat. Because, it came home to him with the impact of a body block in football, that was just what he had been doing. The clearheadedness he had always insisted on—the business of putting his head down and driving forward until he got, not *a* right answer, but *the* right answer, rose up inside him and called him a liar.

"You're right," he said, looking at Peep, Ellen, and Curt. "It doesn't feel right. There's something wrong with it—telling them what they haven't found out for themselves. Some plain, simple reason why not . . ." He stared at Curt and Ellen. "Well, help me!" he said exasperatedly. "You were the ones who had reasons why it wasn't good for me to speak up. Now, tell me why!"

They looked back at him, frowning unhappily, but silent.

"I don't want to be clever about this," Jim ground out. "I just want to be right. There's some reason . . ." He knew he was falling back into the old pattern of going head-down after an answer, but there was not time for him to learn new techniques now.

"Let's see . . ." He scowled, working it out on his own, "You both pointed out how something bad could result from my telling them; but that's negative reasoning. If it's valid, I ought to be able to find positive reasons to back it up. Let's see . . . suppose I tell Llalal now. Then he'll build this no-time transmitter right away instead of later, when his world comes to it on their own. He'll be . . . they'll be suddenly ahead on the knowledge scale without having paid for what they know by working out the in-between steps needed to get where they are . . . without having done the work that proves they could have found it out on their own—" Jim broke off suddenly. "Of course!"

Curt and Ellen looked blankly at him.

"Of course!" Jim repeated to them. "Don't you see? These in-between steps are needed to make sure they really understand the knowledge when they get it. Just as when you're teaching physics or chemistry you make the students repeat the basic experiments that led to the science they already know. Without working out those steps, these Quebahrians, just like science students, would have a hole in the structure of their knowledge. Besides, there may be possibilities in the knowledge they'd miss that we humans overlooked, but the Quebahrians will see as they learn it for themselves. Maybe they'll come up with something we've never suspected, because of their different minds and way of working things out!"

"Why, sure!" said Curt, lighting up. "And not only that—without the experience the Quebahrians will get working out this knowledge for themselves, they might later be blocked from going any further. Or they might be led into some mistake through ignorance that could end up by destroying all three races and the whole planet!"

"Not only that," Ellen chimed in, "but the process of discovery could have a profound effect on their cultural development. If they found out one day that they really weren't responsible for their own technological advance, they might start questioning themselves—" She broke off, turning around. Jim turned to see Llalal striding toward them.

"The time for decision is here," said Llalal, stopping before Jim. Jim nodded and found himself squaring his shoulders.

"Llalal," he said in Quebahrian, "I'm sorry, but I can't help you. I can't tell you why this weapon works and your copy of it didn't. Forgive me, but I'm a failure. Now, don't you and your friends be foolish about this. My friends and I, and the bundii, can stay here while the rest of you escape, and the Noifs may think it was only us who broke in here in the first place—'' He broke off, suddenly, remembering his original reason for wanting to escape with the Mauregs and spun about to face Curt and Ellen once more. "Wait a minute!" he cried. "I didn't tell you. I don't think the beacon will work—''

He broke off, for neither Curt nor Ellen were listening. They were staring up on top of the machine, above all their heads. Llalal was also staring upwards. Jim lifted his eyes.

Peep had climbed up on the weapon. More than that, he had now cranked it around, so that it pointed down at the humans below.

"Peep!" shouted Jim, in English. "What?" But he never did finish what he was about to say.

"Bundii fix . . ." squeaked Peep in his best bundii voice, and shoved the vernier control to the full limit of its scale.

Without warning, it was as if Jim and Curt and Ellen beside him were caught underwater. A heavy, shimmering, liquidlike substance enclosed them, a substance through which raced visible waves of shock like golden lines, to the ringing of sharp, pinging sounds. The substance reached up to enclose even Peep on the weapon above them; and straight ahead through the shifting, distorting distance that separated them, Jim saw the shocked and disbelieving face of Llalal, staring blindly past him.

"—disappeared!" Llalal was shouting, his voice tinny-sounding and far off, through the sound of shifting movement of what enclosed the humans and

Peep. ''Brothers, the three and their bundii have been made into nothingness by the weapon . . .''

The sound and movement of the medium enclosing Jim grew louder and more active. He felt his senses swimming and he drifted off into unconsciousness, feeling himself somehow borne upward on it as he went like a cork released toward the surface by some submarine explosion at the bottom of the sea . . .

14

Jim opened his eyes on soft artificial light and a white ceiling.

He was lying—no, he was sitting, although it was almost lying, in a relaxed position—on something soft. His arms were on soft arm rests. It felt like a chair. In fact, it was a chair.

Jim sat up with a jerk. He was in a lounge, just like the lounge of the spaceship that had brought them all from Earth. Curt and Ellen were sitting up in other chairs and looking back at him with matching bewildered expressions. Peep was standing between their two chairs, beaming at all of them.

"What?" said Jim. For a moment the wild notion crossed his mind that he had dreamed it all, that he had never left this lounge and everything from the shipwreck had been part of his dream.

But then he noticed that Curt and Ellen were still wearing their Maureg clothes and slightly golden complexions, that Curt still had his scalp lock and Ellen her helmet of hair and green eyes.

"Hey!" said Curt, wonderingly, "what happened?"

"Yes," said Jim, looking hard at Peep. "What did happen, Peep?"

"Can't you guess, young friends?" beamed the Atakit. "We have been rescued."

"Rescued?" said Jim.

"But . . ." said Curt, turning to look at the little Atakit, "you shot that weapon at us . . ."

"No, no," said Peep, looking distressed. "I merely pretended to operate the device considered a weapon by the Noifs and Mauregs, so that it should seem to provide a reason to the Mauregs for our vanishing before their eyes."

"Yes," said Jim, pulling himself together. "How about that? What got us up here in this ship—we are in a ship, aren't we?"

"In a spaceship, yes," said Peep. "Returned to it by a rescue device which you, young friend, will probably end up understanding much better than I do, since your interests take a scientific bent while mine," said Peep, looking down his nose modestly, "are merely philosophical."

"Peep!" said Ellen, speaking up for the first time

and looking sternly at the small Alien. "You said
returned!"

"So I did," said Peep, turning to her. "This is, in
fact, the same ship that brought you to Quebahr
although I notice those responsible for the ship have
repaired the wall of the lounge here that I was forced
to tear, and no doubt have also repaired whatever
other damage was necessary to convince you of the
need for abandoning ship."

They all stared at him.

"You mean," said Jim, between his teeth, "it was
all a trick—all a fake—even our being stranded on
Quebahr?"

"By no means," said Peep, solemnly. "Had you
not all made the right decision, you would not have
been rescued. By now you would be dead, or again
in the hands of the Noifs of the Temple City of
Annohne."

He looked around at their silent faces.

"Of course," he said, "we were fairly sure you
would make the right decision. The tests that selected
you to leave your native planet were very reliable,
very reliable indeed. However, the freedom of choice
was always yours. You could have told Llalal about
electricity as a power source, giving the Quebahrians
information they have not yet earned for themselves,
and introducing an alien element into their culture's
logical development toward its future. But," he continued, beaming at them each in turn, "of course you
did not."

"Just a minute!" said Ellen, firmly. "Were we cast away or weren't we? I just want to get that part straight."

"We were cast away, young friends," said Peep, "but by deliberate plan. As I said a moment ago, can't you guess why?"

They gazed at him, almost grimly.

"The Federation wanted to test us!" Curt burst out. "The tests on Earth weren't enough. They had to give us this extra trial—"

"No, wait," said Jim, slowly. He stared hard at Peep. "There was a test involved in this, but it wasn't the important part. The test was like an end-of-semester exam. Am I right, Peep?"

"You are right, young friend," said Peep, happily, "of course, I was sure you would be."

"But we haven't—" Ellen stopped, suddenly thoughtful.

"Yes, we have," said Jim, setting his jaw. "You bet we have. You and Curt and I have just been through first grade of school, Federation style. Isn't that right, Peep?"

"The comparison is not exact, but the implication is essentially accurate," said Peep. "You have indeed been exposed to an educative situation."

"With you as teacher," said Jim, gruffly.

"Oh, no. No. Dear me, no!" Peep's small hands beat the air in embarrassment. "Merely a companion, an observer—at most a sort of quasi-bodyguard.

How could I teach you, young friends? I am myself a student.''

"Studying what?" asked Curt, skeptically.

"But surely you know," said Peep, distressed. "I am, and have been since we met, studying how concern for you, young friends, may prove to be a source of strength to me in controlling the natural violence of my nature.''

Curt gazed at the little Atakit and shook his head bewilderedly.

"I don't understand," he said.

"I do," said Jim, doggedly. "Your current thing-to-learn happened to fit with our current thing-to-learn, so you took the job of looking after us.''

"Not looking after you, young friend . . .''

"Call it what you want," said Jim. "It doesn't matter. The fact is you did look after us and we were cast away on Quebahr to be educated. Now, the question I want answered is, did we?''

"Did we what?" asked Curt.

"He means, did we get educated?" said Ellen, leaning forward in her chair interestedly. "I want to know that, too.''

"I assure you all," said Peep, "I don't know. That is a question you must answer for yourselves.''

They stared at him, once again wordless.

"How can *we* tell?" asked Curt.

"Wait," said Jim, "I've got an idea. Tell me one thing, Peep. Wasn't it a pretty high price to gamble with—the danger we might change the whole future of three races of people on Quebahr—if we failed the test and I talked out of turn?''

"Not quite as high as you think," said Peep, solemnly. "You see, the living culture of a progressing people has a certain protective inertia, or refusal-to-believe. Any new idea, in order to be accepted, must fight for its place by knocking down all the old, false conceptions that disagree with it. Consider, for example, the fact that the Orientals of your world knew of gunpowder before the people of Western Europe, but that it was the Europeans that proceeded to cause a cultural revolution by applying it to weaponry on a large scale. The earlier intellectual inertia of the Oriental resisted the possibilities of the gunpowder concept successfully, but in Europe the concept was victorious."

"But what's that got to do with us and Quebahr?" asked Ellen, sounding fascinated rather than argumentative.

"Merely that this inertia can be calculated," answered Peep. "If our young friend, Jim, had informed Llalal about electricity and its potential as a power source, the idea would have lived briefly in the minds of Llalal and his Brotherhood, but died in the face of the conceptual inertia of the Mauregs as a people, at this era in their history. Only you, young friends, would have been the losers, since you would not have been rescued."

"That's nice!" said Curt, feelingly, "leave us to

die if we fail the test, when we don't even know we're being tested!''

"But young friend," protested Peep. "That is what life is in this universe of ours. Living creatures must grow or die. And to grow each must experiment with the unknown, with a penalty always attached to failure. The experimental physicist," he turned to look slyly at Jim, "walking a shark in a tank. The historical researcher," he turned and bent his glance on Curt, "skin-diving into the past that is the sea-drowned city of Port Royal. The anthropologically minded sociologist who is part of a team camping night after night within a few yards of a gorilla family," he turned finally to gaze at Ellen mischievously, "in the mountains of the Belgian Congo, in order to study their intra-familial relationships during the day: All these take on the risk that the price of knowledge may turn out to be some real, if unknown, danger."

He stopped. Jim, Curt, and Ellen all looked at each other in astonishment for a long moment. Then, they all spoke at once.

"Where's Port Royal?" Jim asked Curt.

"You studied wild *gorillas?*" Curt demanded of Ellen.

"How do you walk a shark?" queried Ellen, staring at Jim.

They all fell silent, looking at each other. Then with one accord they turned to Peep.

"Indeed, young friends," said the Atakit, beaming at them, "you were all most carefully scrutinized before you were selected to study among the stars. First and foremost among the requirements you fulfilled was that of possessing logically inquiring minds. The Federation needed to be sure that you would each try to puzzle out a pattern to whatever events you were faced with after leaving your home world. That you would have your curiosity aroused by as minor an occurrence"—he looked shyly along his nose at them—"as that of allowing Ellen to witness the take-off of this ship from Earth while you other two were hindered from doing so."

The three of them stiffened, and stared at each other again.

"Then there wasn't some special reason for keeping Jim and me locked up that way?" demanded Curt.

"Only the wish to start you puzzling about your situation and its happenings from the beginning," said Peep. "Forgive us for this small deception, young friends. We wanted you to start immediately building a logical explanation for what was happening to you, whether you were right or not."

"I wasn't," growled Jim. "I thought the spaceship wreck and everything after that was caused by a bunch of Aliens among the Federation who didn't want to see us get out to the stars to study, or the human race accepted into the Federation. I didn't even think the rescue beacon would work—that's why I wanted to educate Llalal and his Mauregs, so that the Federation would finally have to investigate, and find us.''

He looked somewhat guiltily at Curt and Ellen.

''I didn't say anything,'' he went on, ''because— well, I didn't think you'd believe me.''

''I did better than that,'' put in Curt. ''I thought it was the Federation as a whole that was trying to make us look bad. So they could use what we did as an excuse to crack down on Earth.'' He rubbed his nose self-consciously. ''I didn't want to worry the rest of you. That's why *I* didn't say anything.''

''I thought the Federation was running a controlled experiment on us,'' confessed Ellen. ''Like a maze test with white rats in a psychology lab. Only life size—with us as the rats and Quebahr as the maze. I didn't say anything because I thought I was the only one who recognized it, from lab work I've done. I didn't want to get the rest of you all excited when you couldn't do anything about it.''

''You see,'' said Peep, solemnly. ''Each one of you theorized. But none of you allowed yourself to be blinded by your theories. When Jim came up with the opportunity of extending the scientific knowledge of the Mauregs—and so upsetting the 'plots' you had each theorized were at work against you—you did not rush to take advantage of the situation. Instead, you began to put together correctly the meanings of what you had seen on Quebahr.''

''Excuse me, Peep,'' said Ellen, firmly. ''But wasn't this all a gamble on the part of the Federation, too?

What if we hadn't run into Llalal? We wouldn't have had any situation to learn from in the first place. Didn't educating us all depend on our getting mixed up in the local situation between the Mauregs and the Noifs—and the Walats as well?"

"It did indeed, young friend."

"Well, then . . ."

"But," said Peep, "there was not so much of a gamble involved as you might think. As one of you"— he looked at Jim—"was fond of saying back on Earth, there is really no such thing as chance or luck in the universe as we presently know it."

Jim started.

"No chance?" echoed Curt. Then he hesitated. "Well, come to think of it, not in history. If you could trace all the causative factors . . ." He let his voice trail off. His eyes were thoughtful.

"Biologically, of course," said Ellen, equally thoughtful, "there's no chance, either . . ."

"Exactly," said Peep. " 'Chance' is a sort of catch-all term for the uncalculated, or incalculable, factors entering into a situation. But the Federation has calculators of great capacity. With these it could be estimated that you would be recognized by the Mauregs as subtly different from themselves. As a result, you would be approached by the Brotherhood, become involved in the Noif-Maureg power struggle, and come to realize what information was lacking to the Mauregs."

"We certainly did," murmured Ellen.

"As the Federation was almost certain you would," said Peep. "On the other hand, we could not be quite so certain that, once you knew the situation, you would make the ethical decision. Yet, despite the 'plots' you theorized were at work against you, when the moment arrived you came to the right conclusion: That your knowledge of the three native races was too limited to justify giving one of them information they had not yet earned for themselves. As a result," Peep beamed at them, "I am happy to inform you three that you have qualified yourselves for Federation citizenship."

"Citizenship!" cried Ellen. They all stared at the little Atakit. "But I thought no humans could be citizens until we invented a faster-than-light drive."

"That is quite true—for your race as a whole," said Peep. "But it must be obvious to you that with an inventive people like you humans, the day of that invention cannot be far distant. When it dawns, suddenly, all of your world's population will be automatically in possession of Federation citizenship, one obligation of which is the exercise of that same ethical judgment you three demonstrated on Quebahr. Consequently, when your world qualifies, it will need the help of those of its own native race in preparing its people to move out among the stars."

"So that's what it is!" said Ellen. "That's what the Federation's after—to educate us so that we can go back home and help train the people who will be using the faster-than-light drive after they find it!"

"Exactly!" said Peep, seriously. "And now you see why it was so vital that you be cast away on a world like Quebahr, to prove beyond a shadow of a doubt that you had the potential, not merely for further education, but for the later job of putting that education to work, once it was completed."

Curt had been brooding. Now he spoke up.

"But you're leaving something out, Peep," he accused. "Why us in particular? What about the seventeen others that were picked back on Earth by the tests?"

"All of them will be facing a situation such as you faced on Quebahr, or its equivalent," said Peep. "However, a number of minor factors, mainly having to do with the cultural background and personality features you three have in common, dictated that you be tested first. The fact was you made an unusually good team. Therefore, you became guinea pigs for all your group."

There was a moment's silence.

"You know, Peep," said Jim, scowling, "there's still something missing here. I asked you earlier if we'd been educated and you said we had to answer that for ourselves. But so far we haven't answered anything for ourselves—you've been doing all the answering."

"That's right!" said Ellen, sitting up sharply. "Why . . ." She fell unexpectedly silent.

"Yes," said Jim, "there's still the matter of what

particular bit of personal education we were supposed
to get from Quebahr. Isn't that right, Peep?''

"Not as far as I'm concerned," said Curt, puzzledly.
"What particular bit of education? I still don't see
any."

"Well, I do!" said Ellen, coming back into the
conversation energetically. "Jim's right. Think about
it, Curt! If it wasn't right to tell the Quebahrians
what they hadn't found out for themselves yet,
then . . ."

Curt frowned, and then suddenly collapsed back
into his armchair, disappearing except for his knees
and the top of his head.

"And I was an Archaist, uniform and all! Of
course, if it's not right for the Quebahrians to be told
things they don't know, it's not right for us—and
that's what the Federation's been up against from the
moment they contacted us!"

He broke off and sat up, looking at Jim.

"You say it, Jim," he said. "You weren't an
Archaist and anyway you were the first one to figure
it out. The honor's yours!"

"Oh, well . . ." growled Jim. He saw them all,
including Peep, watching him and waiting.

"Go ahead, Jim," urged Ellen. "It's up to you to
put it into words for all of us. You're the cleverest."

"Huh?" Jim stared at her. He had never been so
dumbfounded in his life. But they were still sitting,
waiting. Hastily he pulled himself together. "I don't
know why I need to say it out loud if everybody

already knows it," he said, grumpily, "but it's pretty plain the Federation couldn't do much in the way of educating us until we got over the notion that the Aliens were being unfair, or had selfish reasons of their own in not giving Earth any of the scientific advantages they had themselves. At least, until we humans came up with a space drive. Maybe Curt was the only Archaist among us, but I had a chip on my shoulder just the same."

"So did I," said Ellen. "I pretended I was ready to learn from them, but I was really thinking that I wanted to know as much as they did to get even with them."

"That's right," said Curt. "And we couldn't start studying that way. We'd distrust half of what they told us, if not more, looking for some hidden advantage to them in their telling it to us."

"That's it," said Jim. "It never occurred to me that they might have wanted to give us advanced knowledge but weren't able to, for some reason. Not until, that is, I saw what it was like on Quebahr. Then it finally hit me that just as it was for us with the Mauregs, so it was for the Aliens with us. We didn't have the right down on Quebahr to give Llalal and his Brotherhood something that they had to discover for themselves. And the Federation didn't have the right back on Earth to give us what we needed to learn for *ourselves*. It wasn't that they couldn't, or didn't, want to help. They just didn't have the *right* to make our future for us. We have to do that for ourselves, just as the Quebahrians do, and every other race!''

He looked around at Curt and Ellen.

''But the Federation couldn't have told me that before Quebahr,'' he said, grimly. ''Because I just wouldn't have believed them.''

Curt and Ellen nodded.

''Like your race, young friends,'' said Peep, philosophically. ''Like the Mauregs and electricity. Indeed, like myself. We all really learn something when we learn it for ourselves. Love and affection, I have been aware for a long time, are a great aid in the emotional control necessary to the practice of nonviolence. Yet the mere academic knowledge of this has not always deterred me, I am sorry to say—''

''Say!'' cried Curt. He checked himself. ''Oh, sorry, Peep. Go on.''

''Not at all. Go on yourself, young friend,'' replied Peep with stately courtesy. ''You were about to say . . .''

''You said we were just starting our education. Where are we headed now? In this spaceship, I mean?''

''To,'' said Peep, ''a Federation planet which is the fourth world of a star somewhat beyond telescopic range of your Earth. We call the world, vocally, Plieana.''

''—And?'' asked Jim when Peep stopped and showed no signs of continuing. ''What happens there? I mean, to Ellen, Curt, and me?''

''I do not know, young friend,'' said Peep. ''But I

assure you, you will find it interesting." And he beamed at them.

"I'll bet," said Jim.

"So will I," said Curt.

Ellen nodded.

And they all sat silently, thinking about it.

GORDON R. DICKSON

☐ 53068-3   Hoka! (with Poul Anderson) $2.95
   53069-1   Canada $3.50

☐ 53556-1   Sleepwalkers' World $2.95
   53557-X   Canada $3.50

☐ 53564-2   The Outposter $2.95
   53565-0   Canada $3.50

☐ 48525-5   Planet Run $2.75
           with Keith Laumer

☐ 48556-5   The Pritcher Mass $2.75

☐ 48576-X   The Man From Earth $2.95

☐ 53562-6   The Last Master $2.95
   53563-4   Canada $3.50

☐ 53550-2   BEYOND THE DAR AL-HARB $2.95
   53551-0   Canada $3.50

☐ 53558-8   SPACE WINNERS $2.95
   53559-6   Canada $3.50

☐ 53552-9   STEEL BROTHER $2.95
   53553-7   Canada $3.50

POUL ANDERSON
Winner of 7 Hugos and 3 Nebulas

Buy them at your local bookstore or use this handy coupon:
Clip and mail this page with your order

TOR BOOKS—Reader Service Dept.
P.O. Box 690, Rockville Centre, N.Y. 11571

Please send me the book(s) I have checked above. I am enclosing $_____ (please add $1.00 to cover postage and handling). Send check or money order only—no cash or C.O.D.'s.

Mr./Mrs./Miss _____

Address _____

City _____ State/Zip _____

Please allow six weeks for delivery. Prices subject to change without notice.

ANDRÉ NORTON

☐ 54736-5 GRYPHON'S EYRIE $2.95
  54737-3   Canada $3.50

☐ 48558-1 FORERUNNER $2.75

☐ 48585-9 MOON CALLED $2.95

☐ 54725-X WHEEL OF STARS $2.95
  54726-8   Canada $3.50

☐ 54738-1 THE CRYSTAL GRYPHON $2.95
  54739-X   Canada $3.50

☐ 54740-3 MAGIC IN ITHKAR Edited by
  André Norton and Robert Adams   Trade $6.95
  54741-1   Canada $7.95

Buy them at your local bookstore or use this handy coupon:
Clip and mail this page with your order

TOR BOOKS—Reader Service Dept.
P.O. Box 690, Rockville Centre, N.Y. 11571

Please send me the book(s) I have checked above. I am
enclosing $_____ (please add $1.00 to cover postage
and handling). Send check or money order only—no cash or
C.O.D.'s.

Mr./Mrs./Miss _____
Address _____
City _____ State/Zip _____
Please allow six weeks for delivery. Prices subject to change
without notice.

HARRY HARRISON

☐	48505-0	A Transatlantic Tunnel, Hurrah!	$2.50
☐	48540-9	The Jupiter Plague	$2.95
☐	48565-4	Planet of the Damned	$2.95
☐	48557-3	Planet of No Return	$2.75
☐	48031-8	The QE2 Is Missing	$2.95
☐	48554-9	A Rebel in Time	$3.50

KEITH LAUMER